Tyler O'Bannon was flirting with her!

This wasn't like Tyler, but then, Megan was the only unrelated single female at the reunion, so maybe he was bored and practicing on her. She put her hand on his forehead.

"What are you doing?" he murmured.

"Checking your temperature, because you're definitely not yourself!"

"And what is 'myself'?"

Megan lifted her shoulders noncommittally. "I don't know...stern and disapproving?"

"Stern?" His smile made her breath catch. "Do you really think I'm stern?"

"You were. You know, back when we first met. It was obvious you didn't like me. And you sure didn't think I should marry your cousin."

Tyler blinked. Was that *all* she thought had happened nine years ago? No, he shook his head. She must have recognized his attraction to her.

But then, Megan was just a girl when they first met. Not the woman—the *unattached* woman— she was now....

Dear Reader,

As senior editor for the Silhouette Romance line, I'm lucky enough to get first peek at the stories we offer you each month. Each editor searches for stories with an emotional impact, that make us laugh or cry or feel tenderness and hope for a loving future. And we do this with *you,* the reader, in mind. We hope you continue to enjoy the variety each month as we take you from first love to forever....

Susan Meier's wonderful story of a hardworking single mom and the man who sweeps her off her feet is *Cinderella and the CEO.* In *The Boss's Baby Mistake,* Raye Morgan tells of a heroine who accidentally gets inseminated with her new boss's child! The fantasy stays alive with Carol Grace's *Fit for a Sheik* as a wedding planner's new client is more than she bargained for....

Valerie Parv always creates a strong alpha hero. In *Booties and the Beast,* Sam's the strong yet tender man. Julianna Morris's lighthearted yet emotional story *Meeting Megan Again* reunites two people who only *seem* mismatched. And finally Carolyn Greene's *An Eligible Bachelor* has a very special secondary character—along with a delightful hero and heroine!

Next month, look for our newest ROYALLY WED series with Stella Bagwell's *The Expectant Princess.* Marie Ferrarella astounds readers with *Rough Around the Edges*—her 100th title for Silhouette Books! And, of course, there will be more stories throughout the year chosen just for you.

Happy reading!

Mary-Theresa Hussey

Mary-Theresa Hussey
Senior Editor

Please address questions and book requests to:
Silhouette Reader Service
U.S.: 3010 Walden Ave., P.O. Box 1325, Buffalo, NY 14269
Canadian: P.O. Box 609, Fort Erie, Ont. L2A 5X3

Meeting Megan Again

JULIANNA MORRIS

SILHOUETTE *Romance®*

Published by Silhouette Books

America's Publisher of Contemporary Romance

If a woman is lucky, she has three great loves
in her life…her husband, her cat and her cat's vet!
Thanks, Dr. Beachy, for helping make
Gandalf's twenty-one years the greatest.

 SILHOUETTE BOOKS

ISBN 0-373-19502-8

MEETING MEGAN AGAIN

Copyright © 2001 by Martha Ann Ford

Visit Silhouette at www.eHarlequin.com

Printed In U.S.A.

JULIANNA MORRIS

has an offbeat sense of humor, which frequently gets her into trouble. She is often accused of being curious about everything...her interests ranging from oceanography and photography to traveling, antiquing, walking on the beach and reading science fiction.

Julianna loves cats of all shapes and sizes, and last year she was adopted by a feline companion named Merlin. Like his namesake, Merlin is an alchemist—she says he can transform the house into a disaster area in nothing flat. And since he shares the premises with a writer, it's interesting to note that he's particularly fond of knocking books onto the floor.

Ultimately, Julianna would like a home overlooking the ocean, where she can write to her heart's content. She'd like to share that home with her own romantic hero, someone with a warm, sexy smile, lots of patience and an offbeat sense of humor to match her own. Oh, yes... and he has to like cats.

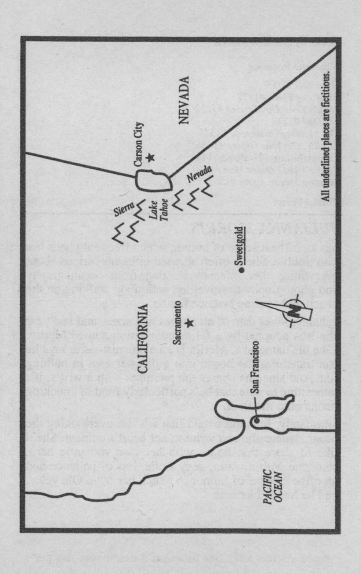

All underlined places are fictitious.

NEVADA

Carson City ★

Lake
Tahoe

Sierra

Nevada

• Sweetgold

CALIFORNIA

Sacramento ★

San Francisco

PACIFIC
OCEAN

Prologue

"He's *so-o-o* terrific."

Megan O'Bannon looked at her seven-year-old daughter and sighed. "Yes, he's very attractive."

Kara turned a page of the magazine she'd mooned over for the past week. Specifically, the article about the *man* she'd mooned over—Tyler O'Bannon, a self-made millionaire with more sizzle than the sexiest movie star. "And he's really related to me?"

"Your father was Tyler's third cousin a few times removed or something. It's a distant relationship—he's never been that close to the family."

"You know, Mom, he *might* come to the reunion if we invite him. He lives in San Francisco, so it's only a few hours' drive."

Megan rubbed her aching forehead. For the past week she'd been planning the O'Bannon reunion, held every three years. The bed and breakfast inn she'd started after her husband's death was the perfect location for the reunion, but things were getting complicated with all this talk about Tyler O'Bannon.

Long-ago memories floated through Megan's head and she closed her eyes. She'd first met Tyler at her engagement party, and something in his dark gaze had made her uncomfortably aware of him...as a man. For a while, Tyler had attended most of the family gatherings, always watching, seeming to disapprove of her. Then he'd just stopped coming.

"Why doesn't he come to any of the family stuff?" Kara asked. "Didn't he used to live with Grandma and Grandpa?"

Megan shrugged. "For a few months. They learned his parents had died and he'd been raised in a group home up north. They brought him to California just before he turned eighteen. But he never really accepted the family."

Kara sighed. "We have to invite him, Mom. He never had kids, so he must be lonely." Her tone made it sound like Tyler was over the hill, instead of a healthy thirty-four years.

"I'm sure he's fine." Megan glanced over her daughter's shoulder at the magazine, and a familiar quiver went through her stomach. The article was titled, "The Sexiest Man in America." And it was right. Even after her lousy marriage and her vow to avoid men, she still got goose bumps when she thought about Tyler O'Bannon.

"Uh..." Kara hesitated. "Grandma Eleanor really wants him to come to the reunion, Mom. And she hasn't been feeling well. It would make her happy."

"Fine, I'll invite him." Megan knew she was being manipulated, yet she couldn't refuse this last argument. She ignored her daughter's jubilation and pulled out some stationary. It had been so long, she couldn't imagine Tyler showing up. But at least it would please Kara and her great-grandmother.

Chapter One

O'Bannon's Inn, Bed and Breakfast.

The sign was lettered in old-fashioned writing, and it hung from a wrought-iron frame. A delicate pattern of morning glories twined around each corner. Beneath it hung a second sign, saying Closed for the Season.

Tyler O'Bannon turned down a tree-lined driveway and saw a beautifully restored Victorian house standing on a small rise of land. There were at least two dozen cars parked in the small lot, and a leisurely game of horseshoes was being conducted in the middle of the garden.

He looked more closely, trying to see if he recognized anybody, but it had been a long time and he'd never known anyone in the family that well, except for Eleanor and Grady. The couple had been kind to him, but angry teenagers aren't particularly receptive to kindness.

A wry smile tugged at Tyler's mouth.

Receptive?

During the months he'd lived with the O'Bannons he'd been a major pain in the behind, with a chip on his shoulder the size of Mount Everest. Too proud for his own good and too stubborn to care.

Tyler parked his Mercedes between a pickup truck and a battered station wagon and got out. In his pocket was an information flyer about the reunion, along with two letters. One was from Eleanor, saying she'd been "feeling poorly lately," and it might be her "last reunion, so won't you come?"

The second letter was from a child, pleading with him to attend the annual family function. A postscript had been added by the kid's mother, saying she was sure he wouldn't be able to fit it in his schedule and not to feel obligated about coming. She'd even written, "I'm sure you don't remember me, but I was your cousin's wife...."

Not remember Megan?

Tyler practically snorted as he headed for the front door of the Victorian. Megan was the forbidden fiancée of his cousin, now his cousin's widow. They'd met at her engagement party, and he'd convinced himself she was marrying the wrong man for the wrong reasons.

For a brief moment, Tyler paused, his hand on the polished brass handle of the vestibule door. He'd like to think he'd come to the reunion for Eleanor's sake alone, but he had to be honest, if only to himself.

He wanted to see Megan again.

Maybe he just needed to be sure she was out of his system, and that things had worked out best for the both of them. She would have been miserable starting out with a penniless husband, and he would have been miserable knowing he couldn't give her the things his cousin could provide.

Right?

"Right," he muttered, knowing in his heart that he wasn't entirely convinced. Shaking his head, Tyler walked through the vestibule into the central hall of the house and glanced around. High overhead hung two crystal chandeliers, lighting the foyer and broad staircase. And, some twenty feet away, a woman was talking to a young girl.

Megan.

And undoubtedly her daughter. For reasons he wasn't willing to examine, Tyler was glad to see that Megan's child resembled her, instead of his cousin.

"We can't put Reece and Jessie in the same room," Megan said firmly. It didn't take a genius to see her patience was wearing thin.

"But they're engaged," the youngster protested.

"I don't know where you get your ideas. Engaged people don't always sleep together."

"Aw, Mom. You're *so-o-o* old-fashioned." Kara rolled her eyes and Tyler couldn't keep from grinning. He'd heard that, between television and the Internet, children grew up fast these days, and Kara was living proof.

"Fine. I'm old-fashioned."

Tyler realized they were so deep in their discussion they hadn't even noticed his arrival. He crossed his arms and focused his gaze on Megan. She'd never been classically pretty, but she had a special beauty that demanded a man's full attention. Five-foot-three, with dark auburn hair and a body that was perfectly proportioned for her petite size. Snug-fitting jeans cupped her bottom and she wore a green T-shirt with O'Bannon Family Reunion printed across the breast.

"We have to assign Reece and Jessie separate rooms," Megan insisted. "Put Reece's fiancée in number four."

Kara looked desperate. "We have to save that room. Because...uh, you-know-who might come."

"He's not coming, Kara." Megan rubbed her temples as if they ached. "Tyler is a wealthy man now. He'll probably think we want something from him. Besides, why would he come after all this time?"

"Because he was invited," Tyler said, deciding it was the right moment to throw his two cents into the conversation.

"Oh, my gosh," the youngster shrieked. "It's *him*. See, I told you he'd come, Mom."

The expression in Megan's green eyes went from affectionately exasperated, to stunned. "Tyler," she whispered.

"Yup, it's me. It's been a long time, Megan."

"You don't...that is, what are you doing here?"

"Don't you remember? You invited me to the family reunion, and how could I resist such a cordial invitation?" Tyler pulled Kara's letter from his pocket and waved it in the air.

"I'll get him one of the shirts," Kara cried happily. She disappeared down the hall.

Megan stepped away, putting the antique reception desk between them. She'd never expected Tyler to actually show up. He *had* kept in touch with Eleanor, calling on her birthday and sending gifts at Christmas, but he'd never visited. Not for years and years.

He's a proud man, Grady O'Bannon always said when somebody asked about Tyler. And Eleanor would finish with, *he'll come back when he's ready.* Eleanor had never stopped hoping Tyler would become part of the family again; maybe her wish was finally coming true.

"Nothing to say?" Tyler asked.

"Plenty." Megan hesitated. It might seem rude, but she needed to understand why he would attend a family reunion after so long. "Why are you here, Tyler? And don't repeat that nonsense about being invited—you've been invited lots of times. And besides, you're always welcome with Grady and Eleanor. You must know that."

His gaze narrowed. "I know. I'm here because I'm worried about Eleanor. She wrote last month and it didn't sound like her at all. It bothered me, so I wanted to check things out," he explained.

Megan nodded. She understood why he'd come back; what she didn't understand was why he'd stayed away in the first place. The O'Bannons were wonderful people—the kind of family she'd dreamed of having when she was a child and her parents were screaming and throwing things at each other.

"This one looks big enough," Kara shouted, running back down the hallway. She waved one of the men's black T-shirts in the air, then thrust it into Tyler's hands. "We made them special for the reunion. Mom did the design."

"Thanks," he said. "You're Kara, right?"

Kara nodded, suddenly shy. "I'm glad you came, Mr. O'Bannon."

"Call me Tyler."

"Okay, Tyler." Kara appeared ready to explode with pleasure, then a shout from outside the house made her feet stir restlessly. "It's my turn for horseshoes," she said. "Do you want to come watch? Or if you want to play, I can teach you how. It's real simple. You have to—"

"I'm sure Tyler wants to get settled first," Megan intervened. "You can visit with him later."

"O-o-okay." Kara reluctantly headed out the door.

"I'll show you up to your room," Megan said, taking the key to room four from a locked cabinet. She glanced beyond him into the foyer. "Don't you have any luggage?"

"In the car. I'll get it later. Actually..." Tyler stopped, his eyes dark and intent. "After what you wrote, I wasn't sure you wanted me to come."

Guilty heat flooded her face. She hadn't meant to sound unwelcoming.

Or had she?

An uneasy shiver crept through Megan and she looked away. Tyler reminded her of things she wanted to forget—of youth and making mistakes and having everything fall apart. Did Tyler know about Brad's womanizing?

About everything?

She drew a ragged breath, wondering if she'd ever get over the sick feeling of her life spinning out of control—of her husband having one affair after the other and finally getting himself killed while driving his fancy sports car.

"You're awfully pale, Megan? Are you all right?"

Tyler sounded genuinely concerned, and she forced a smile to her mouth. "I'm fine. And of course you're welcome. I know Eleanor will be ecstatic. She often talks about you. Grady, too."

"That's nice." He seemed embarrassed by the

comment and Megan lifted her eyebrows. Apparently there were some things Tyler O'Bannon didn't handle with aplomb.

"Well…your room is upstairs," she said.

Megan walked up the broad staircase, all too aware of Tyler following close behind. Nothing had changed since the first time they'd met. He was still too intense, too overwhelming and complicated, while she wasn't complicated in the slightest.

Heck, if she hadn't been exciting enough for her husband, she certainly wasn't any match for Tyler.

Fifteen feet down the hall Megan opened a door and motioned to the interior of the room. "This room has a private bath, so you won't have to share."

Tyler glanced around the room. As in the rest of the house, a scent of beeswax and flowers filled the air, along with glints of light from polished wood furniture and oak paneling. It was a sharp contrast to his condo in San Francisco, dominated by the prior owner's passion for black and white. Though he disliked the stark decor, he'd never taken the time to look for a decorator.

But this…it *felt* like a home, even if it was really a bed and breakfast inn most of the time.

"It's very nice, but it doesn't seem like the kind of place Brad would have chosen," Tyler murmured.

"No." Megan swallowed, and her lashes drifted down, concealing her expression. "I bought the house after the accident. Brad never lived here." She held out the room key, "I'd better get downstairs and check on things in the kitchen. But later we're going to the park for softball, if you're interested in coming."

Tyler took the key, his gaze searching her face. "I'm interested."

"Good. We'll leave in about an hour, so you'll have time to say hello to everyone. I'm sure Eleanor is anxious to see you."

"Thanks." He put his hand on her arm as she started to turn away.

Her eyes flew wide open and she stared at him. "Y-yes?"

"I just wanted to say...you have a beautiful daughter, Megan."

"Thank you."

For the first time since he'd arrived, Tyler saw a natural smile brighten her face. Whatever else, Megan was proud of Kara, and for a bittersweet moment Tyler wondered what it would be like, having a daughter of his own. Having a child with Megan.

Swearing silently, Tyler released Megan's arm and stepped away. It was still there, the sexual attraction between them, along with the knowledge it wasn't going anywhere. He didn't belong with a woman like Megan. She was the princess in the fairy tale, but he wasn't any prince.

"I'll just take a look around, then come down," Tyler said when Megan didn't move. He needed a few minutes to collect his thoughts. At eighteen Megan had been both innocent and sweetly seductive.

She was different now.

The innocence was gone, perhaps understandably. But while Megan was as enticing as ever, the sweet seduction was gone as well. Shadows had replaced the sparkling fun in her green eyes—it was a loss that made him want to cry out in protest.

The door closed behind Megan and Tyler uttered another curse, this time aloud.

He crossed to the window and stared out at the garden. It was full of cheerful O'Bannons, laughing and playing, or sitting and talking. Kara was up at the horseshoe pit, taking aim at the post. After a moment of careful concentration she sent the horseshoe flying. It spun around the target and a flurry of congratulations followed.

Tyler's frown deepened. He didn't known anything about families and he was too old to learn. All the "what if-ing" in the world wouldn't change things. Kara was another man's daughter, and he was what he'd always been—an outsider. Not that he blamed anyone but himself. The O'Bannons had tried, it wasn't their fault he couldn't join their picture-perfect world.

Megan appeared in the garden and crossed to a woman sitting with her back to the house. She knelt and said a few words, then the woman turned, looking directly at his window. It was Eleanor.

She saw him, smiled brightly and waved, motioning with her hand to come down.

Tyler lifted his own hand in return. Eleanor was the closest thing he had to a mother. He should just forget about Megan and concentrate on finding out what was wrong with Eleanor. He might not fit in, but at least he could get the best doctors on the planet to take care of her.

With that thought, Tyler looked at the T-shirt Kara had given him to wear. He flexed the muscles of his left biceps, trying to decide if the short sleeves of the shirt would cover the tattoo he'd got while serving in the army.

He could just imagine Megan's reaction if she saw that damned eagle.

"He said you wrote to him," Megan muttered to Eleanor, still on edge from her encounter with Tyler.

Not that that was anything new. Tyler had *always* made her nervous. It was the way he had of looking at her, as if he had secret thoughts she could never understand.

Eleanor patted her hand. "Of course I wrote to him, Megan. You know, he's such a fine man. I always knew he'd do well for himself. But it's a shame he never married—he'd be so much happier with a wife and family."

Megan's fingernails dug into her hand. She adored her grandmother-in-law, but there were moments when Eleanor was purely difficult. *Like now,* when she got that matchmaking glint in her eyes.

"I don't think Tyler is interested in wedded bliss," she muttered.

"Maybe. But you know...I could tell he was attracted to you back then."

Attracted? Megan automatically shook her head. Not a chance. Tyler didn't even *like* her, much less have any warmer feelings.

"Tyler barely knows me," she said hastily. "And I was engaged when we met."

Eleanor took her hand and patted it. "Megan, you're part of the family now, and you always will be. But Brad is gone. We don't want to see you alone."

The kind words made Megan sigh. She'd discovered there were worse things than being alone—things like having a husband who couldn't be faithful, and who said it was your fault because you weren't woman enough for him. Considering the alternative, she preferred being alone.

"Don't get your hopes up, Grams." Megan gave the older woman a hug. "I'm not interested in getting married again. I know you want more children around to spoil, but you'll have to be content with Kara for the time being."

"Maybe Reece and his fiancée are planning a family," Eleanor said thoughtfully.

Megan doubted it. Reece O'Bannon might be taking a trip to the altar, but she couldn't see him changing diapers and walking the floor with a teething infant.

"It doesn't seem right," Eleanor fretted. "I have three children, six grandchildren, and only *one* great-grandchild."

"You're just jealous of Carolyn," Megan said lightly. "Because she's ahead in the great-grandchild department."

"Hmmph."

Eleanor and Carolyn were twin sisters who had married twin brothers. They were devoted to one another, but that didn't mean there wasn't some healthy competition between them. Especially when it came to grandkids.

"Hi, Tyler," Kara shouted from the horseshoe pit.

Startled, Megan looked up in time to see Tyler smile at the greeting. He'd changed from his suit into black jeans and the T-shirt Kara had given him. If Megan hadn't known better she would have said he was just an average guy, not too different from the rest of the O'Bannons.

"Who am I kidding?" she muttered under her breath.

There was *nothing* average about Tyler O'Bannon. He was taller than she remembered, with broad shoulders, a flat stomach, and long, muscular legs. He didn't carry an excess ounce of fat and he had the natural grace of an athlete. On top of that, he was blessed with naturally wavy black hair and the sexiest smile in human history.

"What's that, Megan?"

"Nothing, Grams."

The corner of Eleanor's mouth twitched. "Of course not."

Tyler walked toward them with an unhurried stride that still ate up the distance quickly. "It's good to see you." He hesitated a moment, then leaned down and gave Eleanor an awkward kiss.

A pleased pink flooded her wrinkled cheeks. "Sit down, Tyler, and tell me how you've been."

"I'm more concerned about you," he said bluntly.

His face had a determined, I'm-getting-to-the-bottom-of-things expression. It was the same expression Megan had found so intimidating nine years ago, and she wondered how Eleanor would stand up to it now.

"Oh…" Eleanor waved her hand about in a vague dismissing motion. "We older folks have our aches and pains. You mustn't pay any mind."

"Your letter—"

"Don't fuss, dear."

If Megan hadn't been watching closely, she wouldn't have seen the nearly imperceptible shake of Eleanor's head, or the way her fingers tightened around Tyler's much larger hand.

What did it mean?

Eleanor was such a strong woman. She worked long hours at the church, rarely complained, and was generous to a fault. If she had one shortcoming, it was her persistent effort to marry off the unmarried members of her family—an effort that extended to widowed granddaughters-in-law.

Megan sat back on her heels, a cold sensation rushing down her spine. What if something was terribly wrong with Grams? The thought was so disturbing that she stopped listening to the conversation. It was only when Eleanor asked whether Tyler liked children that her head shot up.

"Grams," she said, a faint scolding note in her voice.

"Hush, dear. I was asking Tyler a question."

"Please don't get any ideas."

"Now, now." Eleanor gave her a benevolent smile. "Tyler and I are just catching up. Isn't that right?"

"Yes, ma'am." He sounded amused, but there was a wary glint in his eyes.

"None of that 'ma'am' nonsense. You call me Grams, just like Megan."

"Grams," Megan repeated firmly. She didn't want to spend the family reunion fending off Eleanor's matchmaking efforts, much less have Tyler think she was trying to land herself a husband. A *rich* husband, no less.

"Yes, dear?" Eleanor had a look of guileless innocence on her face.

"You...we have to talk," Megan said to Tyler. She jumped up, grabbed his hand and dragged him away.

"Is something wrong?" he asked.

Megan stormed into the living room and tossed her hair over her shoulder. "Of course there's something wrong, or do you enjoy being grilled on your interest in fatherhood?"

"Oh, that."

"What do you mean, oh that?" she demanded.

"Every Christmas Eleanor asks if I've met a nice girl yet. And then she says how nice it would be if I started a family. She's just being polite."

"No," Megan said with a distinct lack of patience. "Grams thinks I should get married again, and since she's so fond of you, she's decided we'd be an ideal couple. And I'm *not* interested in getting married again," she added hastily.

"Tell her."

"It's…complicated. I don't want to upset her, not with her health so questionable."

"Oh, yes." Tyler rocked forward, his attention focused on Megan. She was really worried. "What exactly is wrong with Eleanor? You heard her brush me off when I asked, but I know something is going on."

Megan sighed. "I don't know. She claims she's fine, but her color is bad and she's losing weight. She hardly eats anything, even when I bring her favorite dishes over to the house. Heck, her mother-in-law is doing better than she is."

"Yes…Grandmother Rose," Tyler said slowly. "She turned a hundred last year."

"That's right. We had a big party for her. Invitations went out to *every*one."

He sighed. "I know. I sent a gift."

"She would rather have seen you."

Tyler wanted to believe it was true, that his presence would have been more pleasing than the flowers and fine jewelry he'd sent. But he didn't belong with the family. Grandmother Rose wasn't *really* his great-grandmother, she was a distant relation to him, like the rest of the O'Bannons.

He didn't know what to say to them, and he usually ended up feeling like a buffalo stomping around in a field of clover. Now, after years of perspective and finding success in his life, he was perfectly willing to admit it was his own fault.

"Why didn't you come, Tyler?" Megan asked. "Grams was so sure you'd come for Rose's party."

He couldn't answer, couldn't explain that he hadn't wanted to see her so soon after Brad's death. How could he reveal that the reason that had kept him away was the very same reason he'd come to the reunion?

And the reason was Megan.

Chapter Two

Warning tension crept though Tyler and he shook his head. It was wiser, not to mention safer, to concentrate on something else.

Anything else.

Megan might be a widow now, but she was his *cousin's* widow, however distant that relationship might have been. Tyler cleared his throat, looking for something to change the subject. He finally decided it was the direction of his thoughts that needed changing.

"Look, why are you so bothered by Eleanor's matchmaking?" he asked.

Megan blew a strand of hair from her forehead. "I just don't want Grams getting her hopes up. About either of us."

"Don't worry. I'll only be here for a few days, then things can go right back to the way they were."

"You don't know anything about the way things were," Megan countered. "I mean...not that you *should* know, and I'm not criticizing or anything, but you've been gone and I've been here and…and…," she stuttered to silence.

Interesting.

She looked flustered and tongue-tied, a condition that made Tyler want to smile. "Yes?" he prompted, enjoying this previously unseen side of Megan.

"Uh…that is, I know I'm not blood family, but…" She stopped again and lifted her shoulders in a helpless shrug.

"The O'Bannons don't care about blood ties."

"Then why did…you…uhm…" Megan stuttered into silence a third time and Tyler couldn't control his grin.

"Why what?"

She ran her palms over her thighs in a nervous gesture. "Eleanor mentioned it was a little tense when you lived with them—that you kept saying you weren't really family, and why should they bother? And…well, you did stay away for a long time."

Tyler's grin faded. The issue of his childhood was a sore subject, though not because of the O'Bannons. He'd been raised in a boys' group home, made to feel like a charity case because he didn't have any "family." By the time Grady and Eleanor arrived on the scene his pride had grown to such immense, angry proportions that even an army tank couldn't have put a dent in it.

And what could they have said, anyway? They'd taken him out of duty, not love. He might respect that choice now, but it didn't make any difference.

"Staying away is my concern," he replied stiffly, then kicked himself. The charming, flustered expression on Megan's face vanished and she bit her lip.

"Sorry. But you *did* ask."

"Yeah." Tyler ran his fingers through his hair and sighed. Some things never seemed to change. His pride continued getting in the way, especially in relation to Megan. He couldn't have pursued her nine years ago because of his cousin, but it still rankled to think he wouldn't have had a chance. There was so much that had never been said between them, he was at a loss, not knowing what to say now.

"I didn't mean to offend you," she murmured, sounding more tentative than before. "It means so much to Eleanor that you've come to the reunion. Grady will be thrilled, too."

Tyler looked at Megan, a frown creasing his forehead. He'd built up a lot of ideas about her over the years, ideas about her marrying Brad mostly because he was charming and handsome and belonged to the right social class. He supposed it was a way of protecting himself, because he'd taken one look at Megan at her engagement party and found himself thinking about fairy tales and happy endings.

Impossible endings.

Now Megan belonged to the family in a way he never could, and it was still impossible. "You really love them, don't you?" he asked quietly. "The O'Bannons."

Megan's head snapped back, irritation swamping other emotions in her eyes. "Of course I love them. You don't understand. You never understood," she muttered angrily and not too clearly.

"Understood what?"

"Nothing. It's not important."

"It seems important to you."

She gave him a look that suggested he was a low-level moron. "Go outside and visit with everybody. If there's anyone you don't recognize I'm sure Grams or Kara will make the necessary introductions."

"What are you going to do?"

"Check on dinner." Without giving him a chance to say anything else, Megan hurried away.

It was on the tip of Tyler's tongue to call after her, asking why she didn't have a maid or cook to handle that kind of detail, but he stopped himself just in time. The California Gold Country was a beautiful place and attracted interesting tourists, but bed and breakfast inns were hard work. If Brad had left Megan a ton of money, she probably wouldn't be in the hotel business in the first place.

Tyler whistled under his breath. That was something he hadn't considered. He'd assumed Megan and her daughter were well-provided for, but what if they weren't?

He walked back into the garden and gazed around. The afternoon sun filtered through the trees, putting warmth into the crisp October air. Various members of the family were heading for the house and they stopped, greeting him. They didn't say anything about his long absence, just how glad they were that he'd made it to the reunion.

"Tyler? Has Megan thoroughly warned you off?" Eleanor asked as she stood and draped a quilted lap robe over her arm. "She puts up huge No Trespassing signs, but underneath she's a very sweet girl."

"I'm sure."

Eleanor chuckled at his wry tone. "You never understood Megan, but that's all right. Give it some time."

You never understood....

Tyler frowned thoughtfully. Megan had just accused him of the same thing, or at least of generally not understanding. It was probably a feminine thing. And he couldn't disagree—women were damned hard to understand.

"Tyler?" Eleanor said, putting her hand on his arm. "You do like Megan, don't you? I know she can be prickly, but that's because she's been hurt."

He winced, realizing Megan was right about one thing—Eleanor was matchmaking. "Of course I like her," he said automatically, knowing it was the only answer he could give that wouldn't make things worse.

"Good. It's been hard for her since Brad..." Eleanor's voice shook.

"I know you miss him."

"Mostly I miss what he should have been," she said sadly. "The boy made such a mess of things. Then he got himself killed that way and made things worse."

Tyler's eyes shot wide open.

Brad O'Bannon had been an extremely charming playboy with parents who indulged his every wish. Apparently he'd never changed. He was the one member of the family Tyler had never really cared for, but it was a surprise to hear Eleanor say something critical about her grandson. It also sounded as if there was more to Brad's death than a simple car crash.

"Well, now, look who's here!" Grady O'Bannon exclaimed suddenly, charging across the garden with the energy of a man half his age.

"Hello, sir."

Grady drew Tyler into a hug, thumping him on the back with hearty enthusiasm. "It's good to see you again, lad. We missed you."

"It's good to be here," Tyler said uncomfortably. He was coming to the conclusion it was easier to run a marathon than visit the family he'd never known that well in the first place.

"Tyler," Kara called, offering a welcome distraction. "Mom said to give you time to settle in, but we're getting ready to go to the ball field." She held out her hand with shy anticipation in her eyes. "Are you ready?"

"Sure. Let's go."

"I want Tyler on our team," Kara exclaimed. They'd just arrived at the ball field and the youngster tumbled from the car with more enthusiasm than grace.

"Maybe I'll just watch," Tyler said. "There seem to be more than enough players."

"Oh. But are you *sure?*" she asked. "It's loads of fun."

"Sweetheart, don't pester Tyler," Megan said. "He doesn't have to play if he doesn't want to."

"Sorry."

Kara looked so disappointed that Tyler sighed and found himself agreeing to join the team.

"Yippee! I'm going to tell Reece. He's the other captain." Kara immediately dashed away, heading for the tall, brown-haired man who had arrived at the field ahead of them. They'd come in a dozen different vehicles, most of them filled to capacity. Nobody wanted to miss one of the family softball games, even if they didn't actively participate.

"Isn't Kara a little young for softball?" Tyler asked.

"Anyone who wants to participate, gets to," Megan murmured. "But you don't have to go along just for Kara. I know you aren't used to children and don't play softball that often. Not in San Francisco. Besides, you work in an office with secretaries and stuff all calling you sir. That magazine said you—" The words froze in her throat as Tyler caught her elbow and swung her around.

"So you think that's why I don't want to play? Because of an idiotic magazine article?"

His eyes blazed at her and she swallowed. Well, too bad. Megan lifted her chin. He wasn't going make her tongue-tied and incoherent. Not this time. She tried to shake his fingers away from her elbow, but without success.

"Jeez," she muttered. "You don't have to make a federal case out of it." Maybe if she annoyed Tyler enough he'd leave her alone. It was too confusing having so many different responses to the man. Her body was going hot and cold, her mind was screaming "don't give him an inch," and her heart was in full retreat. Tyler wasn't safe, he was like a panther in the wild—lean and dangerous.

"For your information, my business is property development," Tyler said. "We specialize in restoring old buildings. That's how I started out, buying old places, fixing them up, and selling them. I wasn't born rich and I haven't forgotten how to swing a hammer and work hard."

"Like I said, you don't have to make a federal case out of it," she snapped. "What's wrong with you? I was trying to be considerate, that's all. I love my daughter, but kids can be exhausting and Kara isn't any exception.''

"Sorry.''

She looked at him suspiciously but he seemed sincere. His fingers gentled, stroking the soft inner skin of her arm.

"Did I hurt you?'' he whispered.

"No...of course not.''

"I'm just sensitive about that article.'' Tyler grinned lopsidedly. "I thought the magazine was going to write a real story about the importance of dedication and hard work, instead they made it sound like I did nothing but eat caviar and chase women all day.''

"Not exact—''

"*Mo-o-om,* aren't you guys coming?''

The insistent shout from the softball diamond made Megan jump. "They probably want to get started,'' she said.

"Er...right.''

Tyler shook his head as he followed Megan toward the other players. Lord, he was losing his grip. Two hours of exposure to the woman and he was acting like a raving lunatic. On the other hand, it didn't excuse his behavior, or the things he'd said.

"Hey.'' He caught up in two long strides. "Am I forgiven?''

"Don't worry about it. I'm not.''

The careless answer tightened his gut, but Tyler gritted his teeth rather than say something else he'd regret. It was much harder than he'd expected to pretend Megan didn't mean anything to him. Though...male hormones and pride being what they were, he should have realized seeing her again wouldn't be easy.

Hell, why couldn't she have grown a third eye or something?

Glancing down at Megan, Tyler knew that wasn't the answer. He had a dismal feeling she would attract him no matter what. It was as if she exuded some type of chemical that messed with the normal functioning of his brain.

"You're on our team," Kara said the minute they got close. "I already told Reece."

"I see." Tyler smiled at the child. One of his friends had a daughter close to her age, so he had some experience with kids. Not *that* much experience, but at least he knew better than to ruffle her hair or treat her like an infant. "How good are they?" he asked, gesturing toward the group clustered around Reece O'Bannon.

"We beat 'em two out of three times last year," Grady declared. "Nobody gets a run off one of my pitches."

"Granddad, you know the doctor said you couldn't play so soon," Megan scolded. "You're benched."

"I can pitch. The shoulder is as good as new."

"You don't want to tear that rotator cuff again, so go sit with Grams." She pointed toward the small stand of bleachers with a no-nonsense look on her face.

Grady muttered something beneath his breath about uppity youngsters who thought they knew better than their elders, but Tyler detected a twinkle in the old man's eyes.

"I heard that," Megan said. "And it was your idea to make me captain this year. Now *go*."

Grady retreated, though not before offering another protest.

"Eleanor writes every couple months, but she never told me Grady had had surgery," Tyler said. "He's what—at least seventy-five? How did he get hurt?"

Megan smiled. "He did it golfing, only he won't tell us the whole story. And he's eighty-one."

Tyler looked toward the bleachers and whistled. If he could be that active at the age of *sixty* he'd consider himself lucky.

"All right," Megan said. "Let's get set up." She swiftly gave directions to the team, assigning them positions and a batting order.

Good-natured jeering passed between the two teams, and they tossed a coin to determine who would bat first. Megan's team lost the toss and they scattered to their positions on the diamond.

From his spot at first base Tyler watched her take her place as shortstop. He shouldn't have taken her comments so seriously, but he didn't have good sense when it came to Megan.

He was so deep in thought that the crack of a ball hitting wood made his head jerk around. A teenager he didn't recognize was charging toward first base, determination in each step. There were shouts of "hurry," "run" and "easy out" from all sides.

The right fielder scrambled after the moving ball and threw it in time for Tyler to tag the first out of the game. The next two outs weren't so easy, and they barely prevented the other team from scoring, tagging the runner as he rounded third base, headed for home.

"Told ya we'd get you," Megan told the other captain as they exchanged places on the field.

Reece tugged the braid that had fallen forward over Megan's shoulder. "It's just the first half of the first inning, kiddo. We have six and a half to go."

"I'm not worried. By the way, I like your fiancée," Megan said, nodding toward the slender blond woman by third base. "She seems really nice."

"Thanks." Reece looked uncomfortable for some reason, but there wasn't time to ask questions, so Megan gave him a quick kiss on the cheek. "Don't worry, you'll get used to the idea of being married," she murmured, guessing it might be cold feet affecting him.

"Right."

He didn't sound convinced and Megan supposed she wasn't the most reliable source on the subject of wedded bliss. Most of the family knew about Brad and the way he'd played around. She squeezed Reece's hand, wishing she could promise him happily-ever-after. Problem was, she didn't believe in happily-ever-after. She wasn't sure she ever had.

As for Tyler...Megan watched as he leaned against the fence, ten feet away from the dugout where the rest of the team was waiting. His arms were crossed over his chest and his posture reminded her of someone braced for something.

What?

A blow?

An unwelcome overture from the family? That seemed most likely considering the way he'd never visited. He probably didn't want to get *too* friendly.

A small frown gathered between Megan's eyes.

Tyler confused her; he always had. And his continued resistance to the O'Bannons confused her most of all. Eleanor and Grady loved him and worried about him. They wanted Tyler to be part of the family, but he acted as if they were little more than strangers.

Against her better judgment, Megan walked around the backstop and headed straight for Tyler.

"Why don't you come over and sit with the team?" she urged softly. "The benches aren't that comfortable but it gives us all a chance to visit."

"I'm fine."

His expression said it all. *I'm a loner.* Big and tough and able to take care of himself. Megan turned to join the rest of the family, then glanced into the small rise of bleachers and saw Eleanor smiling and nodding encouragement.

Terrific. Grams was bent on matchmaking and she'd played right into the scheme by approaching Tyler for no reason. At least not for a reason that made any sense.

Sighing, Megan shrugged out of her sweatshirt and tied it around her waist. She wasn't certain whether she liked Tyler, and she was fairly certain he didn't like her, but she could be a good hostess for the next few days. It wouldn't kill her.

"It's a family reunion," she murmured. "Visiting is our major recreation."

Tyler looked at her and she saw layers of emotion in his brown eyes that she couldn't begin to fathom. "People who know each other 'visit.' They talk about their lives and the kids and catch up on news since the last time they were together."

Megan opened her mouth, then closed it just as quickly. Jumping to conclusions would just get her in trouble, and she had a feeling she'd already drifted into deep water. Not that it was a new sensation, Tyler always made her feel out of her depth. After all this time, he still made her feel things she'd rather not think about...things that made her breathless and uneasy in the pit of her stomach.

A chorus of encouraged cries were a welcome distraction and Megan saw that Kara was coming up to bat. "You can do it," she called.

Kara jauntily balanced the bat over her shoulder and Megan's heart filled with love. In many ways Kara was older than her years, yet she was sweet and loving and full of enthusiasm. But time was passing so quickly it wouldn't be long before she was grown. A mixture of pride and pain squeezed Megan's throat and she sniffed.

"Oh, dear," Tyler muttered in a low voice. "What's wrong?"

She blinked away a hovering tear. "Nothing."

"Right." He slipped her a handkerchief. "That 'nothing' is getting your face wet."

He sounded gruff but sympathetic, so she sighed. "It's just that children grow up so fast."

"So my friends say."

It was an innocent comment, but it caught her attention.

So my friends say.

Why did that sound so lonely? A man like Tyler probably had more friends than he could count. Still...friends weren't a substitute for family, she knew that better than anyone.

She looked up and saw him focus on the game

with a kind of hungry intensity. Megan pressed a hand to her stomach, unnerved by more than physical awareness.

"I noticed the pitcher is taking it easy on Kara," Tyler said, motioning toward the mound. "Nice, slow pitches that go straight across the plate."

She swallowed, trying to get control of herself. "I...I know we sound competitive, but this isn't the World Series. It's more important for everyone to have fun than to win," she said finally.

"I see." Tyler nodded, his gaze still fixed on the game.

Kara took a swing at her third pitch. The ball connected with a dull thud and bounced toward third base, just inside the foul line. With a gleeful "hurray," she dropped the bat and ran.

"Go, Kara, go," cried a dozen voices.

Tyler leaned back against his fence and surveyed the field. It was plain the opposite team wasn't reacting as quickly as they did with the older players. They were giving Kara a chance to reach first base. To be a part of the game, just as Megan had said.

He didn't know if child psychologists would approve of their tactics, but it was rather nice. At the same time he would have been furious with the O'Bannons if they'd done anything like that when he was a teenager—he would have accused them of treating him differently, of giving him charity.

Yet all they were doing was being kind.

It was the same round robin of arguments he'd fought since his boyhood, and Tyler tiredly brushed his hand over his face. Coming to the reunion was a mistake. He didn't know how to talk to these people, and Megan still affected him to the point of irrationality. Hell, he would have done anything to wipe the melancholy expression from her face when she was talking about Kara.

"By the way, is there anyone here you don't know?" Megan asked. "It seems strange, I guess, since they're your family, not mine. But you haven't been..." She stopped, looking uncomfortable all over again.

"I'm slowly putting names to faces, though there are a few I don't recognize, especially the kids," Tyler said, ignoring the last part of her statement. They were both tiptoeing around the subject of his absence from the family. "And I haven't seen Rick and Sue yet."

At the mention of her mother- and father-in-law, Megan smiled and shook her head. "They aren't coming. They decided to spend a year at a monastery in Colorado, finding their 'inner peace.'"

Tyler lifted his eyebrows. "I guess they haven't changed." It was a polite way of saying Rick and Sue were just as flaky as ever. Nice, but flaky. He'd certainly liked them better than their son.

Brad...

Tyler's hand tightened into a fist. He kept remembering Brad, probably because his cousin was inextricably connected to Megan, who was alive and standing close enough that his senses were infused with her uniquely feminine scent.

"I..." Tyler cleared his throat. He shouldn't have thought about his close proximity with Megan. It wasn't wise. "Actually, I don't remember that guy," he murmured, motioning to a man sitting among the other players.

"That's Jack Carter. He's an in-law, like me. Hey, Jack," Megan called. "Come and meet Tyler."

Jack came over and gave Tyler an affable grin. "Nice to meet you. My wife is Kara's second cousin, once removed." He looked at Megan and scratched his balding head. "Or is it third cousin, twice removed?"

"Second cousin, Jack. I'm glad you could make it."

The two men shook hands, then Jack walked to the mound and proceeded to strike out spectacularly. He returned with the same friendly expression as before and stood next to Megan. They chatted about his growing family, which was about to increase again. Megan craned her neck and waved to her daughter's second cousin, who'd been benched by eight months of pregnancy. Tyler *did* remember Antonia O'Bannon—now Carter—though she'd changed considerably in the intervening years.

"Your kids are beautiful, Jack," Megan said.

She had the same wistful look she'd had when she'd watched Kara and nearly started crying. Tyler shifted uneasily and tried to think of ways to change the subject. Motherhood was a powerful thing, practically beyond male comprehension, or so he was told. And looking at Megan's beautiful, yearning face, he was willing to believe it.

"Yup," Jack agreed. "My looks and Toni's brains. They got the best of both worlds."

The outrageous statement startled Tyler, then he realized it must be a family joke. Jack was a pleasant-looking fellow, but Toni was so gorgeous she probably stopped traffic on a regular basis. It was one of the things that made him uncomfortable about these family gatherings—not knowing the inside jokes and reasons for laughing.

The inning ended with a single run scored by Kara, who was so proud she nearly burst when she landed on home plate.

They only earned one more run in the next five innings, with four scored by the opposing team. It left them two behind at the bottom of the seventh and final inning, softball being played with two less than standard baseball.

"Okay, we can still do it," Megan said.

"Yeah, tomorrow or the next day," Jack Carter said drolly.

"Ha. A defeatist attitude." She shook her finger with mock severity. "I say we're going to win."

But it didn't look promising when their first batter struck out. The next several plays earned them one run though, putting Tyler on third with Megan on second, and one out left. The next batter came up to the plate, making a big show of warming up. Megan called something from second and Tyler glanced at her, smiling faintly. Her spirit was infectious. He wanted to win the game, just for Megan.

Tyler didn't even wait to see where the ball was headed when the next hit came. He just put his head down and charged for home plate. He hit the backstop, then turned and watched Megan racing for home.

Everyone was shouting and from the corner of his eye he saw Reece O'Bannon bringing his arm up to throw the ball.

"Slide, slide," the team screamed in unison.

No. Tyler cringed at the thought of Megan hitting the dirt. Despite the growing chill in the late afternoon air she'd left her sweatshirt tied around her waist, so there was nothing to protect her arms or face. Not that she would slide. Women didn't get that physical.

Putting on a burst of speed, Megan flung herself forward, hands outstretched. A split second later the catcher had the ball in hand, but not before she'd touched the plate, making the winning run.

For an instant Tyler sagged against the backstop, then he strode forward and hauled her to her feet.

"Are you all right?" he demanded.

"Of course." She laughed and brushed dust from her T-shirt and jeans. A like amount of dust smudged her face, but it didn't seem to bother her.

The rest of the team came out with a victory yell, along with the opposing players who cheerfully offered their congratulations. Tyler accepted his share of the praise, but he couldn't keep from watching Megan.

He hadn't wanted her to hit the dirt, because he hadn't wanted to see her get hurt. Just then something on his hand caught his attention and Tyler looked down. A streak of red kicked the adrenaline in his veins into overdrive.

"Megan!"

He dragged her out of the family group and not-so-subtly examined her for injury. At the sight of a long scratch on her forearm, he scowled.

"Look what you did."

"Oh, pooh." She shook her head. "The cat does worse than that on a good day."

"Then you should have the wretch declawed."

Megan put a hand on her chest. "Sacrilege. Ninety

percent of his personality is in the tips of his claws. It would be like Delilah cutting Samson's hair.''

Tyler didn't want to examine why he felt so protective of her. He'd spent a good deal of his adult life trying not to feel anything at all for Megan, and now his gut was twisted in a knot over a mere scratch. He did a mental calculation of the remaining three days of the reunion and groaned. If she could put him into a tailspin in just one afternoon, he was in serious trouble.

"I suppose the women you know would never slide into home plate,'' Megan said after a moment. Her merry expression had altered subtly, becoming more cautious.

"Actually...no.''

"I'll just have to survive not living up to such a high level of perfection,'' she murmured.

Tyler wanted to explain it wasn't a criticism, but she turned away before he could say anything.

"Grams,'' she called. "I need to go back to the house early. Can you take Kara and Tyler in the van?''

"Of course, dear.''

He watched Megan's departing back and sighed. Considering her impact on him, he ought to be relieved she was angry.

But he wasn't. A part of him want to grab her and make her listen, then kiss her senseless. It wasn't too civilized of him, but none of his feelings about Megan were civilized, so it wasn't surprising.

"Going to do something about that?'' asked a voice and Tyler turned his head.

"About what?''

Jack Carter smiled shrewdly. "About Megan."

Tyler wasn't about to answer. He definitely needed to do something about Megan...he just had to decide what that something might be.

Chapter Three

"That was a grand game," Grady O'Bannon said contentedly. "I'll be out there next year, just got sidelined by this darn shoulder of mine."

Tyler nodded, still amazed that Grady was so active at his age. "I understand you got hurt golfing?"

The white-haired man leaned closer and put a finger to his mouth. "We were racing, and I tipped my cart over on a slope. Don't tell Eleanor, or I'll never hear the end of it. She says I'll never grow up."

"My lips are sealed." Tyler hid a smile and swallowed some more of his coffee. Some things never changed, like Grady and his childlike enthusiasm for life. As a resentful teenager, Tyler had failed to recognize that wonderful quality. As an adult he was suitably impressed.

Dinner had been a delicious Irish stew, crowded with meat and vegetables in a flavorful gravy. Homemade rolls and cornbread had filled out the menu, followed by apple pie and ice cream. Simple, satisfying and easy for a large group.

It was getting late and Grady glanced across the room to where his wife and Megan were finishing a board game with Kara. At the same time a shadow crossed his face; Grady frequently looked at Eleanor—often with concern, always with love.

Tyler had tried pumping him for information on Eleanor's health, but it seemed Grady was as much in the dark as the rest of the family.

Worry turned in Tyler's chest and he sighed. He'd maintained contact with the elderly couple, but always on his terms. They'd respected his wishes, and now it was probably too late to change things.

"Well," Grady said, "I hate to be an old fogey, but we'd better follow everyone to bed."

"Good night, sir." Tyler shook hands with the older man.

Eleanor persuaded a yawning Kara to join them as they headed for their rooms upstairs, leaving Tyler alone with Megan. The casual way they'd been left together didn't surprise him; Eleanor might not be feeling in top form, but she was still a matchmaker of the first order.

Megan didn't say anything, she just busied herself with putting the game back in the box.

"That was a delicious dinner," he said, mostly to make her look at him.

"It's all from Eleanor's recipe file. She taught me to cook after Brad and I were married."

"You didn't know how?"

"No, I didn't." Megan slapped the lid on the game with unnecessary force. "Believe it or not, cooking isn't programmed into the female brain, it's something you have to learn.''

Over the years Tyler had developed an instinct for trouble, for knowing when things weren't exactly the way they seemed. And something told him there was more to Megan's vehemence than a knee-jerk feminist reaction.

"I was just making conversation," he murmured.

Across the room he could see her take a deep, calming breath. "Sorry."

"That's okay, I owe you one after getting uptight over the magazine article."

"The article wasn't so bad," she said.

He snorted. "The Sexiest Man in America? I could strangle that writer."

Megan thought there were worse things than being called sexy—like not *being* sexy. She wiggled her fingers, noting the short, practical nails and chapped skin from working in the kitchen and garden. But it wasn't so bad, she was Kara's mother, which counted the most. And she belonged to a terrific family, even if it was only by marriage.

"People write articles to sell magazines," she said absently. "Kara has six copies of it stashed under her bed. And she and her friends have your picture taped to their bathroom mirrors."

"Ohmigod. You aren't serious, are you?"

The groaning note in Tyler's voice brought Megan's head up and she smiled faintly.

"Afraid so. But don't tell Kara I told you. She'd be mortally embarrassed. And it's no worse than boys drooling over pictures of half-naked models and actresses. Anyway, it's the age they're at—you

know, the age between birth and college gradua-
tion?''

"I wouldn't be a kid again for all the money in
the world.''

"Me neither," Megan whispered. She hadn't enjoyed any part of her childhood, so she was determined to give Kara as many happy, carefree years as
possible. But it wasn't easy, not for a fatherless child.

At least Kara didn't know everything about her
father, she hadn't been old enough to really understand the way things were. And Megan had made
sure Kara had never heard her parents fighting.

"I want to apologize about what happened at the
game. I wasn't criticizing," Tyler said slowly. "It
just surprised me that you didn't make a fuss over
getting hurt. Some women would have worried about
it leaving a scar.''

She gave Tyler a startled glance. "It was just a
scratch, and we were having fun.''

"These days the women I know don't get excited
about much of anything. They're too sophisticated.''

Sophisticated.

Megan carefully set the game box onto its proper
shelf. One thing was certain, she wasn't sophisticated. She'd tried to fit into Brad's circle of wealthy
friends, but it had never worked. After a while she
hadn't cared very much, even when he criticized her.
And he was always criticizing. According to Brad
she was too innocent, too straightlaced...too *boring*.
Never enough of a real woman to satisfy him.

Pushing the painful memory away, she took a tray
from the antique sideboard and began gathering up
the various cups and plates around the room. The
O'Bannons liked to eat, almost as much they enjoyed

visiting with each other. They wandered in and out of the kitchen at all hours.

To her surprise, Tyler took another tray and joined the process of cleaning up after the evening's festivities. At one point they both reached for the same cup and their hands accidentally touched.

Megan sucked in her breath, shocked by the awareness shooting through her body. She didn't want to be aware of Tyler. It wasn't a new conclusion, but it needed constant reinforcement. Men and romance weren't a part of her future. She'd blown one marriage, she wasn't foolish enough to try a second time.

She hastily crossed to the opposite side of the room and straightened the cushions on the couch, spending an unnecessary amount of time on the task.

"This is a great house," Tyler said after a few minutes. "But I remember it was a wreck the last time I drove through the area. Who did the restoration?"

"I did."

"You?" Tyler asked, startled. Once again Megan had surprised him.

"With a lot of help from the O'Bannons," she added. "It's amazing what you can do with paint, hard work and muscle power."

"It takes a whole lot more than paint."

He looked around the room, his practiced eye envisioning the work it had needed. Why would a woman like Megan buy a broken-down Victorian and do the work herself? And why would she start a bed and breakfast inn? So far, his trip to the Gold Country was leaving more questions than answers in his mind.

"That kind of restoration is pretty expensive. Plumbing, wiring—everything must have needed redoing from the ground up."

"Just about."

Megan walked to the door opening into the central foyer and gazed up at the crystal chandeliers. She knew Tyler was wondering about money and how she'd afforded everything, but she didn't intend to discuss it with him.

As for the house…she'd always wanted the old Victorian, from the first time she'd seen it. It was a house where children had grown up safe and happy, a place with history and roots and beauty. Brad had laughed at her for wanting such an old-fashioned place in the country, but she'd still dreamed about living there one day.

And now it was her home.

A fond smile curved her mouth as she remembered everyone showing up with power sanders and paint sprayers, sheets of drywall and table saws, laughter and support. They'd brushed her protests aside, coming every Saturday for months until the task was done. She'd finally insisted they would have the next family reunion at the house, as a way of saying thank you.

"You have a nice family, Tyler." She looked back at him. "They don't care that Brad is gone, they still treat me like I belong."

"You do belong."

Megan shrugged. Most of her belonged, but there was a part that still wasn't sure—largely where Tyler was concerned. He was the niggling thread of uncertainty, the disapproval that hovered in the background.

Maybe it didn't even come from Tyler...maybe it was her own doubts. What kind of woman looks at a stranger and imagines what it would be like to touch him...to have him touch her? At her own engagement party?

"You didn't approve nine years ago," she said finally. "You made it clear how you felt."

"I never intended..." His protest trailed into silence and the expression on his face became strained. "Honestly, I didn't disapprove of you."

"Forget about it."

"Megan, you do belong," he said swiftly. "I can see how much you love everyone. And here you are, hosting the reunion. You're part of the family. Certainly more than I've ever been."

"It was your choice."

Tyler clamped his jaws shut. He didn't want to argue, not tonight. There was too much to think about and he'd already said too many things he regretted.

"It's different for you, Megan. You have a real place in the family," he said at length. "You're a daughter-in-law...the mother of a grandchild. It's not that clear-cut for me."

She looked at him curiously. "That isn't true, you're—"

"I know. I'm a blood relation. But it's hard feeling any connection when you're a distant cousin ten times removed."

"It's a little closer than that."

"Not by much."

The emptiness in Tyler's words made Megan shiver. He'd always seemed so blamed independent she'd never realized he might be lonely at the same time. Was it all an act? A defense to keep the hurt of not belonging at a distance?

"Tyler..." she whispered. If only he could understand how much the O'Bannons loved him and wanted him to be a part of their lives. It was what they'd wanted from the beginning.

All at once he smiled, the dark shadows vanishing from his face so thoroughly she wondered if she'd seen them at all. "Never mind, Megan. And please don't look so melancholy, you're making me feel guilty."

There it was again, his veneer of being so self-sufficient, of not needing anybody. It was that very confidence that had made her tongue-tied in the past, but now she was seeing more of the man beneath.

And liking him too much, darn it.

"I don't want you to feel guilty," she said, squaring her shoulders and pushing less comfortable thoughts to the back of her mind.

"Good. You always were a nice little thing."

Nice?

Little?

They weren't descriptions destined to bolster her ego, but Megan swallowed her pique and lifted her chin to match her squared shoulders. Maybe *like* was too strong a word. Maybe what she meant was that she understood Tyler better now.

"Why, thank you. But I'm not little. I'm very capable."

"Well, you've sure done a lovely job on the house."

Megan's pulse jumped at the warm approval in Tyler's eyes, which went to show she didn't have a shred of good sense.

''Oh, please.'' She rolled her eyes and motioned to the reflective strips on her sweatshirt and shoes. ''I light up like a Christmas tree in headlights. I'll get some for you, too.''

''That's all right. I'm too big for a car to miss.''

''You should still wear something. It's safer.''

''But—''

''Do you know what Grams would do to me if I got you killed?'' she demanded, darting back up the steps.

''Nothing,'' Tyler declared, but she didn't stop. He smiled ruefully and waited. If he hadn't already been wide-awake, the sight of Megan in her running shorts would have brought him instantly to attention. It was a response he'd be wise to ignore.

But it was hard to remember such good advice when she returned and began pinning reflective tape to the back of his sweatshirt. The thought of Megan's slender fingers touching other portions of his anatomy was a temptation he didn't want to pursue, so when she turned her attention to his chest he stepped back.

''I'll take care of this part,'' he said, taking the tape and pins.

''There's a lot of going up and down,'' Megan murmured as she did a series of warm-up stretches. ''You might not like it. It's hilly here.''

He glanced at her from the corner of his eye. ''I live in San Francisco, remember? I know about hills. We're one of the hilliest cities in the world.''

''Oh. Right.'' Faint pink invaded the skin on her neck, and he wondered whether the blush had started from her breasts and moved up. Hardly the kind of thinking to keep him out of trouble, but he was in a reckless mood this morning.

"Shall we go?" he asked.

By unspoken agreement they walked down to the road, where the surface and lighting was better. The grass was rimed with a hard white frost and Tyler took a deep breath. In San Francisco the air was permeated with the scents of the city, even in Golden Gate Park. This was much better.

"It's great," he said softly. "Do you always run so early?"

Megan shrugged. "I usually wait until it's light, but when the family is here I go earlier."

"Is it safe for you to go alone?"

"Safe enough." She did a couple of warm-up stretches, then started out in a steady stride.

Talking wasn't practical, so Tyler concentrated on watching the unfamiliar road. Megan ran faster than he'd expected for such a small woman and he settled into the pace with a satisfied nod. Running was his release, a means of dealing with tension. It helped him focus in a way that nothing else could. More than one of his problems had been worked out on a morning run.

On the return leg of the run they stopped to drink water from a roadside water fountain.

"You don't have to go faster, or further, than usual," he said.

"I'm not."

Tyler looked at Megan. She was breathing quickly and beads of perspiration dampened her forehead, but she wasn't distressed.

"If you want to do more, don't let me hold you back," she added. "I'm used to running by myself."

"Trying to get rid of me?"

Her gaze flew to his and he saw confusion, followed by irritation. Yup, she certainly had the temper of a redhead. He shouldn't have teased, except "shouldn'ts" were hard to remember when she reacted so fervently.

"I just thought you might prefer going faster," she replied tartly. "Your legs are longer than mine."

"Hey...I'm sorry."

Tyler touched her damp cheek. He was being crummy, but things were getting interesting. A long time ago he'd turned his back on the complications of family and feelings he couldn't handle. Maybe this time he should stick around long enough to figure out what was really happening.

"I tease too much," he murmured.

"Yes, you do." But a reluctant smile tugged at Megan's mouth. Tyler was an O'Bannon, all right. They were champion teasers, and he was obviously just warming up.

"So, how did you know I'd be running this morning?" Megan asked as they approached the house. There was only a faint touch of light on the horizon and they still had to walk carefully up the driveway.

"Eleanor mentioned it. She said you were a real early bird."

Hmm.

Grams was definitely matchmaking.

Dumb move, Grams.

Megan stuck her chin out. Her hair was damp and she was breathing hard—not exactly a romantic condition. She tried to be glad, but her feminine ego was healthy enough to wish she had the cool poise of

Grace Kelly. She'd bet no one had ever caught Grace with a sweaty face and no makeup.

Inside the main house it was still quiet, though the faint sound of a television came from the carriage house. The O'Bannons with young children had elected to stay there during the reunion, where they could have a separate place to put the youngsters down for naps or quiet time. And since Megan had dedicated one of the rooms as a rumpus area, the kids seemed to be loving it.

"Better get a shower fast," she warned Tyler as they climbed the staircase. "Everyone will be getting up soon, and there won't be enough hot water to go around, not with this crowd."

Tyler grinned. "So it's every man—and woman— for themselves?"

"Something like that."

"It sounds serious," he said, lowering his voice. "We could save water and shower together. I'd be happy to scrub your back."

The sexy teasing temporarily robbed Megan of her voice. This wasn't like Tyler, but then, she was the only unrelated single female at the reunion, so maybe he was bored and practicing on her. After a long minute she swallowed and put her hand on his forehead.

"What are you doing?" he murmured.

"Checking your temperature, because you're definitely not yourself!"

"And what is 'myself?'"

Megan lifted her shoulders noncommittally. The words that came to mind weren't particularly flattering. "I don't know...stern and disapproving?"

"*Stern?*" Tyler wrinkled his nose in an attractive

manner. Of course, everything he did was attractive, so a cute nose wrinkle wasn't surprising. "I don't like *stern*. Can you come up with something else?"

"Not unless you do," she retorted, determined not to succumb to his charm *or* her nerves around him.

"Hmmm. Do you really think I'm stern?" His smile made her breath catch.

"You were. You know, back when we first met." Megan lifted the hair on the back of her neck, still warm from her exertions. "It was obvious you didn't like me. And you sure didn't think I should marry your cousin."

Tyler blinked, unsure he'd heard right. Was that *all* she thought had happened nine years ago? No, he shook his head. She must have recognized his attraction to her. Most women jumped to that conclusion, whether it existed or not, thinking every man must want them. And Megan...

He froze, struck by a new realization.

Woman?

Or a child, becoming a woman.

When they'd met, Megan was just eighteen. And, while some teenagers are experienced by that age, Tyler had a growing suspicion she hadn't been one of them.

"Tyler? Are you conscious?" A pair of fingers snapped under his nose and he looked at Megan in shock, wondering how many of his ideas were going to be demolished this weekend.

Logical or not, he'd always felt Megan had chosen between him and Brad. But if she never realized how much she affected him, then he'd been wrong all this time.

Lord. He'd thought endlessly about Megan.

Dreamed about her. Been furious with her. Railed against fate and the impossibility of wanting another man's fiancée, and now he was confounded all over again.

Breathing faster than he had at any time when they were running, he shook his head. Nothing had changed, yet everything was different. His one defense against Megan had been that illogical sense of rejection. Without it, he was in serious trouble.

Of course... Tyler ran his gaze over Megan, seeing the healthy flush on her skin and strands of auburn hair curling damply on her temple...some kinds of trouble were more interesting that others.

Chapter Four

"**I**s something wrong?" Megan asked.

"Like what?"

"Just...nothing." She shifted uncomfortably beneath Tyler's watchful eyes. After running for several miles she really needed a shower and change of clothing, yet something in his expression seemed filled with masculine approval.

Which was ridiculous.

If Tyler was looking at her with something more than boredom it was due to the lack of available women.

Stop it.

Megan closed her eyes, wishing she could go back to the time before her marriage, when the hardest thing she had to decide was what outfit to wear to school...a time when she was confident of herself. She'd never believed she was the most beautiful woman in the world, but she'd never had reason to doubt her appeal to the opposite sex.

It wasn't so easy anymore. Now she automatically looked for other reasons to explain a man's interest, or even his smile. And it was so tempting to think Tyler was interested.

"Megan?"

She blinked, realizing he was looking from her to the end of the hall and back. "Yes?"

"There's a furry foot sticking out from under your bedroom door."

She looked down the hall and saw her cat's determined paw stretched out, his claws snagging the throw rug in an attempt to drag it through the narrow space. A low sound like the hum of angry bees was coming from behind the door, which rattled from the force being exerted on it.

"Uh...that's Beelzebub."

"Beelzebub." Tyler's eyebrows shot upward. "Isn't that another name for the devil?"

"He's mostly black, so I thought it fit." Megan went to the door and opened it. Tyler was making her nervous again and she knew she could count on Beelzebub to take center stage.

Beelzebub strolled out—all sixteen pounds of him—looking regally annoyed. He took one look at Tyler and opened his mouth in a war cry. *"Marrorrwwww."*

"Holy cow. He certainly sounds like a devil."

"Never insult a woman's cat." Megan lifted the feline and stroked his long silky fur, but it did little to appease the annoyed animal. He'd been locked up and he didn't like it one little bit.

And he liked seeing her with a strange man even less. Beelzebub was nothing if not possessive. It wasn't quite the same as having a demanding lover in her life, but it was better than nothing.

"I wasn't insulting him," Tyler denied. "How could I—he's gorgeous. What breed?"

"Long-hair domestic."

Tyler's forehead creased. The tone of Megan's voice, more than her words, suggested it was joke. "Long-hair domestic?" he repeated politely.

"You know...alley cat."

"I see." Tyler grinned.

"Actually, he's part Siamese. You can't see his points unless he's in sunlight, but his paws and head and tail are a darker black than the rest of his body," she explained, sounding breathless. "I used to bring his mother food when I was running. She was a feral cat who lived in the hills and I could tell she'd had kittens. Then one day I found Beelzebub in the spot where I always left the food. He was so wild I had a terrible time getting him home."

"What happened to mom?"

"I don't know, I never saw her again." Megan's expressive face looked sad and Tyler again fought an urge to grab her, to promise anything to erase that unhappy look in her eyes. "But at least I have Beelzebub," she said.

Tyler raised his hand, and the feline opened his mouth in a wide hiss. The gleaming length of his fangs was enough to discourage him, and Tyler decided he'd wait until Beelzebub had calmed down before he initiated diplomatic relations.

But it was a rewarding sight, watching Megan cuddle the large black cat. She'd pulled her hair loose from its ponytail, and fiery locks tumbled over her shoulders and around the feline. Beelzebub batted at the bright temptation, yet his claws remained sheathed. Apparently he reserved his wilder instincts for other people.

"He seems fond of you," Tyler observed.

"As far as Beelzebub is concerned, there are only two living creatures that matter—him and me," Megan said, shifting the feline's weight. "Much to Kara's dismay, he won't have anything to do with her. But he enjoys playing with mice, even if they aren't equals."

Tyler smothered a laugh. He doubted the mice appreciated Beelzebub's idea of "play."

"As far as that goes," Megan continued thoughtfully, "I'm not sure he considers *me* an equal. He may just be tolerating my presence. Or as Eleanor says, he knows a sucker when he sees one. She says I can't refuse him anything."

Tyler envied the cat.

He wouldn't mind being petted the way Megan was petting Beelzebub. A grin tugged at the corners of his mouth and he rocked forward on the balls of his feet.

"So...," he said softly. "I suppose I'd have to grow fur and a tail for you to cuddle *me* like that. You know—run your fingers through my hair, rub my tummy...and anything else you'd care to soothe."

Megan's eyes narrowed and she set Beelzebub on the ground—probably to keep her hands free for slapping his face. "I'm sure there are plenty of women willing to cuddle you without fur and a tail. I'm a poor substitute for your legions of lady friends."

"I don't have legions of lady friends." He reached

out and twined a strand of auburn hair around his
finger. Some things were worth a slap in the face.
"Right now, I don't even have *one* lady friend."

"That's hard to believe."

"All too true. I've been celibate for months." His
smile was warm and intent, seeming to exclude everything but the two of them...especially the women
she'd accused him of knowing. "I'm a lonely man.
Aren't you going to take pity on me?"

Megan's heart skipped unevenly, and her gaze
shifted hurriedly up and down the hall. What was the
harm in a kiss? Yet even as she formed the question
in her mind, she knew the answer.

Plenty.

"Lonely? That's a little hard to believe," she
scoffed. "What's the matter? Did you swear off
women and decide to become a monk?"

An inexplicable look flashed crossed across Tyler's face. "No, I'm healthy and still interested in the
opposite sex, it's just..." He shook his head. "The
women close to my age all seem to be developing a
yen for babies. They keep talking about the biological clock."

"Maybe you should date younger women."

He grinned. "*You're* younger."

Megan bit her tongue. "It can't be that bad. The
other women, I mean."

"No?" Tyler shook his head in disgust. "My last
date decided I'd be the perfect sperm donor for a
baby. That's pretty bad—we'd only known each
other for an hour and a half."

"Oh..." Megan clapped a hand over her mouth to
smother a laugh—his indignant expression was price-

less. She cleared her throat. "Did she mean sperm donor as in...a...a doctor's office?"

"No. She thought we should just jump into bed and let nature take its course. But she was willing to sign papers releasing me from any paternal responsibility."

"Big of her."

"Talk about silly notions." Tyler waved his hand around, apparently forgetting his attempt to kiss her. Megan didn't know whether she should be relieved or annoyed with his short attention span.

Though...maybe it wasn't so short after all.

Somehow he'd maneuvered them through the door and into the middle of her private sitting room. A private sitting room was a much more sensible place for a kiss than a hallway. Especially with fifteen or twenty relatives in the house who could interrupt them at any moment.

"You should think of it as a compliment," Megan pointed out. "Her wanting to have your baby and all."

"Yeah, right. I should have known she was up to something from all the questions she kept asking," Tyler growled. "She had this theory that we'd make a superhuman baby together. What does she think I am, a genius?"

No, a stud.

Megan didn't voice her opinion aloud, but she understood the poor woman's point of view. Tyler would make beautiful babies with the right woman. Or any woman. His jeans were filled with the right...genes.

Tyler didn't need money to attract women, all he had to do was *breathe* and they'd fling themselves into his arms. He was a gorgeous, heart-stopping, too-yummy-to-be-believed, genuine hunk, and she was crazy to even consider kissing him.

Reluctantly, Megan stepped backward and tugged at her damp sweatshirt. "We'd better get those showers right away. I can hear someone walking around upstairs, which means there's going to be a mad rush for the bathrooms."

Tyler watched her for a long minute, then nodded. "Yeah, I'm sticky from that run. I'll see you later."

"Later," she whispered.

He closed the door behind him and Megan sank onto a soft love seat. Her body ached with a confused blend of anticipation and frustration. She was tempted to go out and run another few miles to release the tension, but there wasn't time.

"Mrrroww." Beelzebub rubbed against her, his satisfied purr rumbling in the quiet room. As males went, he was jealous, smug and supremely confident of his superiority.

Megan lifted the feline, hugged him close then set him on the bed. She couldn't let Tyler get to her. No more getting into a situation where she wanted him to kiss her. *No more playing with fire.*

Going into her private bath, Megan pulled her running clothes off and dropped them in the hamper. From long habit she didn't look in the mirror. There had been too many times her husband had made her feel inadequate as a woman. Inadequate as a lover.

Her reflection was a reminder of those days.

Impatiently, she closed the shower door and washed her hair. Beelzebub sat outside the shower, keeping up a running feline commentary. He'd lived with her for nearly two years and still didn't understand the peculiar ways of humans. Especially when it came to showers—all that wet stuff was a mystery to the cat mind.

Water dripped onto his nose when she stepped onto the bath mat, and he darted from the room with a loud "Mrrrooow."

"Sorry, baby." Megan held the towel to her, still feeling an edgy throb in her breasts and stomach. "Drat Tyler O'Bannon, anyway," she muttered.

The man was a menace. Death to a woman's peace of mind...and her body. He was just playing a game, flirting to pass the time. She wasn't dumb enough to take him seriously.

Right?

But when she went to her closet, Megan hesitated for a long minute. She had three choices, practical, sophisticated, or the softly feminine dresses she preferred most of all—the ones her husband had disdained, saying they made her look like Rebecca of Sunnybrook Farm.

The "sophisticated" dresses were out, she planned never to wear them again. Sooner or later she'd get around to donating them to the church rummage sale. But she ought to wear something practical, Megan argued to herself, suitable for running around cooking breakfast and lunch.

Suitable.

Something inside deep inside of Megan rebelled at the thought. She'd done everything possible to please Brad, but it was never enough. From now on she was going to suit herself, and let everyone think what they wanted.

Tyler was seated comfortably at a table when Megan walked into the kitchen. Her damp hair was plaited into a French braid that hung to the middle of her back, and it contained the rich shades of autumn...deep red threaded with glints of gold. On any other woman he would have suspected the color came courtesy of an expensive salon, but not with Megan.

He was almost sure she would have kissed him, but it was the *almost* that had stopped him. Just then Megan stretched—arching her slender body with the grace of a silky cat—and Tyler whistled silently.

He liked the soft, feminine lines of her dress. Megan had always worn dresses, he remembered. Soft, pretty things, with long, wide skirts that had made a man fresh out of the army sit up and take notice. Tyler didn't have any complaints about the women he'd served with, but army fatigues couldn't compete with Megan.

"Hot or cold water?" he asked, knowing she hadn't seen him sitting in the breakfast nook.

Megan jumped and spun around. "What?"

"Did you get enough hot water?"

"Sure." She smoothed a strand of hair from her forehead. "You?"

"Plenty."

That is, there *would* have been plenty if he'd used hot water. A cold shower had temporarily relieved the sexual tension in his body, but it wouldn't last if he kept thinking about Megan. He'd known women who were more classically beautiful, but none of them were like her.

"So what happens with this family reunion thing?" he asked. "Any special plans for the day?"

"More family arrives. More games are played. *Lots* more food is eaten, and we'll probably go to the park for another softball game. Nothing too exciting, but we enjoy it."

"More family?" He couldn't keep the astonishment out of his voice. There were already over thirty O'Bannons in attendance. "I know this place is huge, but where are you going to put them all?"

"Some are staying in a local motel," Megan said. "And the carriage house in the back is converted to living space. We used to do the reunion over a two-day weekend, then we started gathering on Friday. This time I told everyone to come on Thursday, if they could."

"And you love it, though it means more work for you."

"Of course I love it. Anyway, we share the work."

They might share the work, but Megan seemed to be doing more than her share, even if she was the hostess. If they had had their reunion at a hotel, there would be employees who were paid for cooking and cleaning. Nobody would have to do anything.

Still...Tyler looked around the inviting kitchen and decided to keep his mouth shut. He didn't have any right to comment on where the O'Bannons held their reunion, and he didn't know enough about families to understand, anyway.

A thunderous sound of footsteps came down the back staircase, followed by Kara dashing into the kitchen. "I'm starving," she declared.

"You're always starving." Megan smiled and pointed to the refrigerator. "So we'd better get started on breakfast."

Kara whirled toward the refrigerator, then saw Tyler. A shy look spread across her face. "G'morning, Tyler. Would you like some coffee?"

"Sure."

Kara got the coffee, spilling some in her eagerness. The cup she set in front of him was so full he could see why she'd left a trail of brown spots across the floor. "Do you want cream?" she asked.

"No, thanks. This is just right." Tyler wasn't sure how he'd drink from the cup without spilling it himself; adding cream would just make the problem worse.

"Sweetheart, will you start setting the table?" Megan gave her daughter an armful of place mats, then discreetly passed a thick wad of paper towel to Tyler. When Kara left the room Megan knelt and wiped up the floor with more towels.

"I should do that," he murmured. "It was my coffee."

"It's part of a mother's job description—we launder, iron, fold and wipe up messes."

"I think you do a little more than that."

Megan deliberately kept from looking at Tyler. She had an awful lot to think about...like why he was teasing her and being so nice. Unfortunately, she didn't have time to think about anything. The O'Bannons would be appearing any minute and the rest of the day would turn into the happy, noisy chaos that she usually enjoyed.

At the sink Megan rinsed her fingers, then stood for a moment, staring out the window at the garden. She didn't have much experience with flirting, so she could be wrong about what happened earlier. Tyler might be just teasing, and she might be trying to make something out of nothing.

Wishful thinking? she wondered wryly.

If it was wishful thinking, then she had self-destructive tendencies she'd never realized before. Romance was not a part of her future. It was something she'd accepted when her husband died—not that her life had been all that romantic prior to his death. Brad hadn't touched her for months before the accident.

"Tell me something," Tyler said, taking a cautious sip from his brimming cup. "The reunion is so close to Thanksgiving. Why have it now, instead of later in November, for the holiday?"

"This is the big reunion that includes the extended family," Megan murmured. "It's every three years."

"You mean it includes distant relations, like me."

He said the words with an even, cool tone, but Megan suspected there was more behind the words—and the man—than she could have imagined. Never in her wildest dreams would she have guessed Tyler was sensitive about the subject of family, that he felt the same needs and longings she'd known as a child.

But she should have.

A shaft of sorrow went through her with the thought. No matter how much money Tyler had made, no matter how successful he was or how many friends he had, he didn't really have anything without a family.

Sighing, Megan opened the refrigerator and pulled out the casserole pans she'd gotten ready the night before. Cheddar cheese, egg and green chili casserole was her bed and breakfast's specialty, along with muffins and wild blackberry jam. The ovens were already preheated, so she put the pans on the racks and set the timer. With an ease born of practice, she sliced ham onto the griddle and mixed muffin batter.

"You should come to Thanksgiving dinner this year," she said after a few minutes. She didn't know what to say about "distant family," she just knew Tyler was an O'Bannon, even if he wouldn't accept it. "It's going to be at Eleanor and Grady's place."

An expression she couldn't read flickered across Tyler's face, then vanished. "Thanks, but I have plans."

Irritation warred with softer emotions in Megan. She was quite certain that Tyler *didn't* have plans, and she was equally certain that deep down he wanted to attend the holiday gathering. He was just too stubborn to admit it.

"It wouldn't kill you to cancel those 'plans,'" she muttered. "And it would make Eleanor happy."

"I don't want to inconvenience anyone."

"What inconvenience? There's always a mountain of food. We love to eat."

Tyler eyed Megan's petite frame. How did someone who "loved to eat" stay so slender?

"I'll think about it," he said.

"Pleeeeze come to Thanksgiving," Kara begged. Neither of them had noticed her standing at the door of the kitchen, clutching a handful of silverware and listening to the conversation. "Mummy makes the best pie, and Grandma fixes a pink punch with raspberry sherbet. It won't be any fun without you."

The extravagant statement sent a warm sensation through Tyler. He'd never realized how refreshing children were. Their joys and pleasures were so immediate, right now Kara really believed it *wouldn't* be any fun if he didn't attend the holiday feast.

"Wow...that sounds great," he said, neither committing himself, or saying no.

But it seemed to satisfy Kara, who gave an excited hop, then went back to her task of setting the table for breakfast.

"Mummy?" Tyler asked softly so the youngster wouldn't hear. "I haven't heard her call you that before."

Megan looked past him, into the dining room at her daughter. "She used to call me mummy, then she started school and got too grown up. But it still slips out when she's upset or she forgets herself. Or when she wants something."

"And you miss it."

The corners of her mouth turned down, then she laughed ruefully. "Yes, but I can't keep her little forever—much as I'd be tempted to try."

"It always surprised me that you and Brad didn't have more children. You used to talk about having a dozen," he said carefully.

The humor faded from Megan's eyes and she shrugged. "Things don't always turn out the way we think they will." She lifted a long-handled fork and turned slices of ham on the griddle.

With a simple gesture she'd shut him out, and Tyler frowned impatiently. "What did I say?"

Across the room he could see Megan take a deep breath, then let it out. "Nothing."

He walked closer, out of easy earshot from Kara in the other room, standing next to her at the stove. "We both know that isn't true. What did I say?"

Megan closed her eyes for a brief moment, then looked at Tyler. In many ways they were alike, though she was only beginning to see the similarities.

No matter how much he protested, he wanted to be a part of the O'Bannon family—he just didn't know how. It had been difficult for her in the beginning, too, but at least she hadn't been fighting pride along with her insecurity.

Of course, that didn't mean her pride wasn't getting in the way *now*. Nobody enjoyed admitting their marriage had been a disaster.

"Megan?" Tyler prompted.

"It turned—" Her voice cracked and she shook herself. Getting worked up over the past was ridiculous and wouldn't change a thing. "It's nothing, really. It just turned out that Brad and I wanted different things. I don't think he enjoyed fatherhood."

"Then he was an idiot. Kara's a great kid."

The flat, unequivocal statements made Megan smile. "I admit to being prejudiced about my daughter. And she was a sweet baby, except when she had colic. Then she was deafening."

Tyler snitched a sliver of ham from the griddle and popped it in his mouth. "Bad, huh?"

"Let's just say you needed earplugs for your earplugs," Megan said dryly. "An ambulance siren was less piercing. She has the lungs of an Olympic swimmer."

"I'm glad she's past the colic stage, then."

"So am I...most of the time."

One of the oven timers went off and Megan took a rack of muffins out, tipping them out onto a cutting board. The fragrant scent of fresh-baked bread filled the air, and she saw one of Tyler's hands edging forward.

"Cut that out." She swatted his fingers with an oven mitt, but not quickly enough to stop him.

Tyler's eyes crinkled with laughter as he tossed the purloined muffin from hand to hand, trying to cool it. "I'm just trying to help."

"Yeah, right."

"You sound skeptical."

"That's because the masculine half of your family is pretty helpless in the kitchen," she drawled. "At least when a woman is around to take care of it for them."

Tyler tried not to laugh. "You mean…they enjoy being waited on?"

"That's one description for it."

He didn't want to know what the other description might be, but he appreciated Megan's fond exasperation. She understood the nuances of the family so well it was an education to watch her. "If the women do the cooking, what do the men do?"

"Watch football," said a voice from behind them.

Megan looked up. "Morning, Grams. I thought you'd be up earlier."

"Grady wanted to sleep in…with company." She winked.

Company? Tyler sensed his jaw dropping and clamped his mouth together. Was Eleanor saying she and Grady had been amorous? As in making love to one another? He looked at Megan, who didn't seem surprised.

"What's the matter, Tyler?" Eleanor asked, then chuckled. "I may be seventy-six, but all the parts work. What's that old saying? There may be snow on the roof, but there's still a fire in the hearth?"

His skin turned hot. "Sorry. I didn't mean to seem…"

"…shocked?"

"Yeah," he admitted.

"I think you're still seeing us from a teenager's vantage point," Eleanor said, not the least perturbed. "Convinced that anyone over thirty is tottering around on a cane, too blind to even notice the opposite sex, much less want to do something about it."

"Hey, *I'm* over thirty," Tyler protested.

Eleanor's head shook sadly. "You're over the hill, then. Time to go into an old folks' home."

"And he's obviously too aged to notice the opposite sex," Megan added. "He mentioned having some kind of problem earlier, but I had no idea things were so serious." She took a pat of butter and cut it into Tyler's muffin, an impish grin on her lips.

"Now I'll totter off and take my morning nap," Eleanor said. She pretended to be leaning on a cane, moving slowly and painfully from the kitchen.

"What about breakfast?" Megan called after her.

"Just toast and tea for me. My aged digestion is so touchy, you know."

Megan frowned, concern replacing the laughter in her eyes. "Actually…toast and tea *is* all you've been eating these days."

"You worry too much, child."

Tyler looked from Megan to Eleanor, storing the interchange in the back of his mind. If he had to personally drag Eleanor to a specialist in San Francisco, she was going to get the medical care she needed. No matter what she said, something wasn't right.

"I do *not* worry too much," Megan mumbled.

"Oh, yeah?" he asked, though her comment was plainly rhetorical since Eleanor had disappeared.

"Yeah."

"Well, you certainly don't worry about skewering my dignity." He cast a glance at Megan. "And about that 'problem' you mentioned, it has nothing to do with a lack of interest in the opposite sex. And I'd be delighted to personally demonstrate whenever you say."

Megan's pulse quickened and a curl of warmth unfurled in her chest. Surely she wasn't so much out of practice that she could mistake the invitation in his gaze or the flirtatious suggestion in his voice.

It thrilled her.

It worried her.

But most of all, it scared her. At best, it was idle flirting on Tyler's part, but even if he was genuinely interested in something more, she wouldn't know what to do, or have the nerve to do it.

Nothing about Tyler was quiet or safe or easy. She'd be smart to avoid him completely, but since that wasn't possible, she would have to ignore him. It couldn't be that hard, could it? There was plenty of family at the reunion to provide a buffer. No one would even notice.

Just then Eleanor poked her head back in from the dining room. "Megan, dear, ask Tyler to help with the barbecue for lunch."

"I don't need—"

"Nonsense. You're doing too much. I'm sure Tyler is happy to help. Aren't you, Tyler?"

"Yes, ma'am," he said obediently, a wicked smile dancing in his dark eyes. "I'll be happy to help Megan."

So much for the family providing a buffer between

them. If Eleanor had anything to say about it they'd be married by Sunday and she'd be pregnant by Thanksgiving.

Now why didn't that sound so bad?

Chapter Five

"**I** have everything in hand, Tyler. Go help Megan. She's the one who's working too hard."

Megan groaned. The person who had "everything in hand" was Bethany O'Bannon, one of Kara's cousins. She was also one of Eleanor's much-lamented *un*married grandchildren. Aside from her single status, Bethany was beautiful, talented, intelligent and obviously joining in with the general fun of matchmaking. Megan wanted to strangle her.

Tyler's gaze met hers from across the garden, then he walked toward her through groups of chattering family and bunches of running children.

"Bethany says I should help you," he murmured.

"I don't need any help."

"Really?" He lifted one eyebrow.

Nine years ago that searing look would have made Megan quake in her shoes. Now it was only mildly unnerving. "Really. I have everything under control."

"Everyone thinks you're working too hard," Tyler said. "I think they're right." He took a carrot stick from the relish tray she'd pulled tight against her stomach and bit into it. "What else needs to be done?"

"Hardly anything. You even cleaned the barbecue grill for me," she growled.

"I'm glad to...help." His voice lowered on the last word, making it sound sexy and suggestive, something that didn't bear any relationship to the dirty, grimy job of scrubbing a barbecue grill!

Megan plunked the relish tray down on the food table and turned on her heel. She felt like she'd been running all morning...mostly running from Tyler. Whether it was by his own design or because of the matchmaking antics of the O'Bannon family, he was utterly unavoidable.

Inside the house everything was quiet except for the grind and crunch of the three electric ice-cream freezers churning in the kitchen. With the mild weather they'd been having, everyone preferred to visit and play outside in the fresh air. Megan poured a fresh supply of crushed ice and rock salt into one of the buckets, then gazed out the window, grateful for the quiet respite.

In the past two years her life had settled into a comfortable routine—family, Parent Teacher Association meetings and taking care of bed and breakfast guests during the summer season. The O'Bannons had urged her to start dating again, but dating was the last thing on her mind.

Or it had been, until her daughter had decided Tyler was the next best thing to chocolate sundaes. Pain twinged in Megan's head and she pressed her fingers, cold from the ice, against her temples.

"Headache?"

She jumped a foot and spun around, narrowly missing slugging Tyler with her elbow. "What?"

"You seem to have a headache. Is there anything I can do to help?"

"*No,*" she said vehemently. She was getting sick and tired of that darned word. Tyler could make *help* sound like anything from doing the dishes to building a crackling fire for an intimate rendezvous.

"You've been rushing about all morning. Maybe you're hungry. That would give me a headache."

Tyler hid a smile as he stepped around Megan. One of the freezer motors was running unevenly, straining, indicating that the ice cream within was sufficiently thick. With a few deft motions he pulled the electric plug and unfastened the top. The ice cream inside was a pale shade of pink, studded with frosty red strawberries.

"This looks great," he said. "I love strawberry."

"I...uhm, grew them in the garden. I froze the berries this spring so we'd have them for the reunion."

"After all that hard work, you should be the first to get a taste." He scooped a frozen chunk of strawberry onto his finger. "Open up."

Her mouth dropped open, he suspected more from shock than any attempt to be cooperative, and he let the fruit slide onto her tongue. They stared at each other for a long moment, unmoving, the tension so strong it was hard to breathe.

"It's customary to chew," Tyler whispered finally.

Megan chewed once and gulped the morsel down her throat. "This is insane. What are you doing?"

"Feeding you. Want another bite?"

"No." She backed hurriedly away, much to Tyler's disappointment. He would have sworn she was as aware of him as he was of her.

"In that case, we'd better cover it up again." Tyler shrugged and put the lid back on the freezer. If he'd had time to consider his actions he probably wouldn't have pushed her quite so hard.

He desired Megan with an intensity that had only grown over the years. But he was equally certain that he couldn't have her. He wasn't right for Megan. She was love and light and family, he was a nobody, as far as family was concerned, who led with his chin the majority of the time. The most he could offer her was money, and money wasn't important to a woman like Megan.

Even as his thoughts crystallized, Tyler sighed.

Nine years ago he'd thought Brad was what stood between him and Megan. But it wasn't his cousin at all, it was *him*. And he'd spent those years making his fortune and trying to think it would have made the difference with Megan, when it wouldn't have made a shred of difference in the first place.

"You look grim," Megan said quietly.

Grim.

Terrific.

The night before she'd called him stern and disapproving. His image wasn't improving in the slightest.

"I'm not grim. I'm...thoughtful."

The description seemed to please Megan because she chuckled. "Okay, you're thoughtful," she agreed. "Now, are you going to *think* about visiting with your family, or will you continue your silent, square-jawed routine?"

"I do not—"

"Yes, you do," Megan said before he could get the protest out. "Just relax. You might discover you enjoy being with the family—visiting and stuff."

"There are some other things I'd like more," he muttered.

"What? Nobody would mind doing something new."

"I'm not talking about large group activities, I'm talking about a little one-on-one action, in private. Something the two of us could do on that great big king-sized mattress upstairs in your bedroom."

Frustration was loosening his tongue to an unwise degree, a fact that was obvious from the shock on Megan's face. Then something happened that he didn't expect...she laughed.

"Megan?"

"You love to tease, Tyler. I never realized that about you before."

She thought he was teasing? Or was this her way of brushing off a stupid sexist remark without getting into an argument? His eyes narrowed as he watched Megan unplug the remaining two freezers. They were sitting on a sloping counter that drained into the sink, and each was different—two older ones, battered with age and use, one newer.

"I thought you had to crank ice cream by hand," he said, deciding it was a safe topic for conversation. And far less frustrating than having her think he was teasing, when he really wanted to drag her off to bed for a year or two.

"Electric is easier, but for the purists, we have three hand-crank models going out by the horseshoe pit."

"I didn't know there were purists when it came to ice cream."

Megan sent him an amused glance. "Absolutely. Grady swears it doesn't taste right if it's churned with a motor. On the other hand, Eleanor loves electric freezers. She wanted one for years, then finally bought one, wrapped it up and gave it to Grady five Christmases ago."

A choked laugh escaped Tyler's throat. "I'll bet he loved that."

"Grady loves *everything* about Eleanor, but he still won't eat machine-cranked homemade ice cream." Megan turned back to the waiting buckets. "We have to get the paddles out of the ice cream, or later it'll be harder to serve," she said over her shoulder. "Then we pack it with more ice and salt, so it can ripen."

"Ripen? How can ice cream ripen?"

"You know, it gets harder and the flavors sort of meld together." She used a rubber scraper, working the ice cream from the first paddle, then smoothing down the surface so she could put the lid back on.

Another stupid sexist remark hovered on the tip of Tyler's tongue, but he managed not to say anything.

"Here, you get the paddle." Megan held out the plastic object, still generously crusted with ice cream, and he looked at questioningly.

"What do I do with it?"

She blinked. "Lick it off, of course. Usually there's a dozen kids around, wanting first dibs. I think somebody must have put a spell on them today, because I haven't gotten a single request.''

Tyler took the paddle, a smile growing on his face. ''Just lick it?''

''Well...yeah. It's no fun to use a spoon. Only you'd better stand over the sink or you'll get it over both you and the floor.''

Megan was obviously in a ''mother'' mode, but it didn't bother Tyler. He stood over the sink and swiped his tongue across the first bit of strawberry cream. The icy bite melted quickly across his tongue, faster than commercial ice cream, tasting so delicious he was astonished.

''I didn't realize...this really is good,'' he mumbled, catching a glob melting off the end of the paddle before it was lost in the sink.

''You must have eaten homemade ice cream before.''

''Nope.''

Megan watched perplexed as Tyler ate the treat, patent pleasure on his handsome face. She didn't know what she'd expected when she'd offered it to him, she'd done it without thinking. During the past two summers she'd often made ice cream for her bed and breakfast guests, and somebody always got to lick the paddle. It was a tradition.

Outside the window Megan saw Kara and she held up a second ice-cream-laden paddle, waving it in invitation. Kara gave a small hop and dashed for the kitchen door.

''Yummers,'' she said, joining Tyler at the sink.

''Is yours peach?'' he asked.

''Uh-huh.'' Ice cream dribbled down her chin and dropped onto her family reunion T-shirt.

"It looks good."

"Have a taste." Kara generously extended her paddle, and without a second's hesitation Tyler gave it a swipe with his tongue.

"You're right, it's great, but I think I like the strawberry better. Try it." He extended his own paddle, but Kara wrinkled her nose.

"Can't. I get a stuffy nose from strawberries."

"Gee, that's too bad. Your mom said she grew the berries herself."

"We grew the peaches, too, so it's all right. We have a great big chest freezer and we freeze all kinds of things. Mom likes to grow stuff."

"You're lucky to have such a special Mom."

Megan's hands shook as she finished packing the second bucket with ice and salt. Kara was starved for a father's attention, and in two minutes Tyler had shown more attention to her daughter than Brad used to show his own child in a month. Brad was never interested in being a daddy. She'd foolishly assumed he would change once they started having children, but it turned out to be one more thing she was wrong about.

As for Tyler's compliment about her being a "special mom?"

It was disturbing as well, but she more easily dismissed it. He was being nice to Kara. He certainly wouldn't say anything negative about her mother.

The third paddle came out laden with vanilla ice cream, and since there were still no other takers, Kara and Tyler decided to split it between them, taking turns cleaning off their respective halves.

It was remarkable how Tyler could have so much fun and still be so gorgeous he took her breath away.

Megan tried to see the aloof loner in him, but at the moment he was just plain sexy, laughing with her daughter and eating ice cream with boyish enthusiasm.

"I wonder where everybody is?" she pondered aloud.

"Grandpa Grady is doing card tricks," Kara said between licks.

"Is that so?"

Since everybody knew there was ice cream churning in the kitchen, the absence of eager children and adults pretending-not-to-be-interested couldn't be explained by "card tricks." She remembered more than one occasion when they'd ended up eating ice cream first and the meal second. The O'Bannons didn't hold to dietary rules when they were enjoying themselves.

Oh, yes. The family was matchmaking with a vengeance.

"I'm going to go play horseshoes, Mom," Kara said as she finished. "And Grandpa started the chicken on the barbecue. He said we can eat in a half hour."

"I thought he was doing card tricks."

Kara stood still, guilt spreading across her small face. "Uh...he was."

"And barbecuing at the same time." Megan took a dishcloth and ran it under the faucet. With swift efficiency she cleaned her daughter's sticky skin. "Okay, you can go play horseshoes now."

Kara scooted out of the kitchen even faster than she'd arrived.

"What about me?" Tyler murmured. "Don't I get your personal attention for the clean-up phase of this ritual?"

Except for a small spot on his perfect chin, there wasn't any need to "clean up," but Megan blandly held out the dishcloth. "Be my guest. You're old enough to manage without personal attention."

"Not even for my first time?"

Since Megan had a wild desire to lick the sticky spot on his chin instead of using the cloth, she wasn't about to get closer to Tyler. It would be *too* dangerous. She'd never had this kind of reaction to a man before, not even to her husband. Tyler made her feel hot and melting inside, empty and needy and drawn to him.

Even the memory of Brad's impatience with her shortcomings as a lover wasn't enough to quell the heat in her stomach, or to quiet the ache in her breasts.

"I'd rather have your help, Megan." Tyler's fingers fastened around the arm she still held out, holding the damp dishcloth. Gently, carefully, he lifted her hand until the towel touched his face, then he rubbed his chin back and forth on the cloth.

Just pretend he's one of the kids.

Yeah, right, proclaimed her alter ego.

Megan tried focusing her attention on Tyler's chest, but that was a mistake. It reminded her of how strong he was, and how nice it would be to cuddle up to him. She doubted he was a cuddler, though. He probably liked his women to be *very* sophisticated in bed, as well as fast off the mark sexually—a description she'd never fulfill.

"You seem upset," Tyler said after a moment.

She swallowed, still not willing to look at him. "I'm fine. I just…wondered how someone could get to your age without ever eating homemade ice cream.''

He released his hold on her arm. ''Nobody I know makes it in San Francisco, and it wasn't on the menu at the home where I grew up.''

The home.

The hollow tone in Tyler's voice told Megan more than the words. He'd only lived with Eleanor and Grady for a few short months, the rest of his childhood had been spent in a boys' group home. She tipped her head back, seeing the cool shadows that had crept into his eyes. What would it be like, not having any cozy traditions, like licking an ice-cream paddle? She didn't imagine a group home offered much more than basic room and board and supervision.

And why hadn't somebody adopted Tyler? He must have been a beautiful little boy. A thousand couples should have wanted him as their son.

''Never mind, Megan,'' he said gently.

''Mind?''

''Everything.'' Tyler smiled again, the shadows disappearing from his eyes as quickly at they'd appeared. ''I enjoyed the ice cream.''

''I...I hope you didn't ruin your appetite.''

''Oh, my appetite is just fine.''

''Good. Grady's won cooking contests with his barbecued chicken, you know. It would be a shame if you couldn't enjoy eating some.''

Tyler managed a wry smile as Megan took him at his word. She didn't play or flirt or assume his comments had sexual implications, no matter what he said or how he said it. She treated everything as a joke, or figured he was only teasing. Some teasing.

No matter how often he told himself that he wasn't the right man for Megan, he still wanted her.

"I'll enjoy the chicken. But to be honest, I'm wondering about that business of Grady cooking. According to you, the male half of the family doesn't cook," he said.

Megan grinned. "I said they were helpless in the kitchen. But barbecuing is more manly than mere cooking. And it isn't done inside. I'm sure it satisfies some deep-seated male need to char meat over an open fire."

"Ah, I see."

"I think it's an atavistic throwback to caveman days," she mused. "Barbecuing probably reminds guys of that old 'ugh, me man, you woman' lord-of-the-cave feeling."

Tyler clasped his hand over his heart. "I'm skewered."

"I doubt that."

"How about slightly stung?"

Megan shook her head. "You're tough. You'll survive." She looked uncomfortable for a moment. "I'm sorry everyone is running you ragged. They all seem to have thrown in with Eleanor on that crazy matchmaking idea of hers."

"It's crazy, all right."

"Absolutely." Megan nodded her agreement, but Tyler frowned.

They'd both agreed it was crazy for anyone to think about pairing the two of them. He knew his own reasons, but what about Megan? Was she still in love with Brad? Devoted to his memory? The thought wasn't palatable.

"For the record, why is it crazy?" Tyler found himself asking.

"It just is."

"That isn't an answer."

Megan shrugged and pulled out a large bowl of potato salad from the refrigerator. "We'd better get the rest of the food out if the chicken is close to being ready."

An impatient frown crossed Tyler's face. He didn't want Megan to brush things off, he wanted an answer. "Why, Megan? We're two healthy, single adults. Why is it so crazy for the family to think about us getting together?"

Megan angrily thrust the bowl into his arms. "Because I was lousy at marriage, that's why. Now take that outside and leave me alone."

In shock, Tyler carried the potato salad out to the food table. He set it down, and stared at the cellophane-covered bowl as if it could give him some answers.

I was lousy at marriage....

He couldn't imagine Megan being lousy at anything, much less marriage. She was sweet and loving and generous. A wonderful mother. The O'Bannons adored her. What could she possibly have done wrong? She was practically perfect.

Okay, he was somewhat partial to Megan, Tyler acknowledged silently. She represented everything he'd ever wanted, he'd naturally have trouble seeing her in any other light.

But lousy at marriage?

Not a chance. She'd be the perfect wife for any man. The real question was, who'd be the perfect husband for Megan?

Megan came out the back door carrying another large bowl. She brushed past him without saying anything, and immediately headed back to the house after setting it on the table with the rest of the food.

Tyler sighed and followed. If nothing else he wanted to be on speaking terms with her.

"Megan, we have to talk," he said as she opened the commercial refrigerator again.

"We have nothing to talk about."

"Yes, we—"

"*No.*" Her face was filled with hurt and wounded pride. Her marriage obviously wasn't something she'd ever intended to discuss with him or anyone else. "We've said enough."

"That's purely a matter of opinion."

She put several containers out on the counter then closed the refrigerator door and sagged against it.

"Okay. Suffice it to say you were right" she said, though she seemed to be talking more to herself than to him. "I shouldn't have married your cousin."

"I never thought you shouldn't marry Brad," Tyler protested, though it wasn't true. He'd thought she should marry *him*, not his cousin. And all the good sense in the world hadn't been enough to persuade him otherwise.

"Fine. Have it your way." Megan straightened, grabbed another bowl and headed outside with it. Tyler followed, cursing his big mouth.

Several members of the family called a greeting and joined in, bringing the last pieces of the meal outside. With more than fifty adults and children attending the reunion, the business of feeding everybody was a huge task.

"Hope everybody's hungry," Grady called, carrying the first platter of barbecued chicken to the table. "'Cause we got plenty."

Standing to one side, Tyler watched as the happy throng jostled toward the table laden with food. There was laughter and friendly jokes about leaving enough food for everyone else, and acknowledgement that, as usual, Cousin Daryl had gotten to the head of the line first.

Tyler leaned one shoulder against a tree and wished with all his heart that he could truly be part of it.

Across the yard Megan pressed a hand against her roiling tummy. It wasn't Tyler's fault that he'd pushed the wrong buttons and upset her, though she didn't know why he kept pushing them. They'd agreed they weren't suited for another, which should have ended the discussion.

Male ego, she decided finally.

He probably didn't like the idea that she wasn't interested. And she *wasn't* interested...much.

Now Tyler was standing, broad-shouldered and solitary, still not participating, and she couldn't stand it. She walked around the picnic tables and pointed toward the food line.

"Go get in line," she said.

"How about you?"

"Oh...I can wait."

"So can I." Tyler patted his flat stomach. "I ate all that ice cream, remember?"

He smiled and she relaxed. With the family within ear shot, he probably wouldn't raise any uncomfortable subjects—like her rotten marriage or the question of their mutual *un*suitability.

"I thought you said the ice cream didn't ruin your appetite," she said lightly.

"Not a chance. It just means I can pace myself and not rush the table."

"Hey, Megan," called someone from the mingled group filling their plates. "Do you have any cracked pepper?"

"Just a minute and I'll get it," she called back. But before leaving she looked at Tyler again. "Do you stand back when your employees are having a party, or do you join in and talk to them?"

"We talk, I guess," he murmured.

"What about?"

Tyler shrugged. "The weather, world news...their families. The usual stuff."

"Then pretend Aunt Sue is your secretary and talk to her about the 'usual stuff,'" Megan said, mildly exasperated. "Get in line and if someone asks about the glories of French architecture, you can wow them with your knowledge."

A smile crinkled the corners of Tyler's eyes. "I don't know anything about French architecture."

"That's okay, neither do they."

"So you're saying I should just dive in?"

Megan grabbed his arm and gave him a push in the direction of the food line. "That's exactly what I'm saying. You aren't shy, so stop acting like you are."

Her task accomplished, she headed for the relative peace of the kitchen, only looking back once she'd gotten inside the doorway. Tyler was holding a plate that someone had passed down the line to him, and was listening to Jack Carter expound about something. Jack was good at talking; he'd talk to a lamp-post if no one else was available.

Megan shivered, her fingers still tingling from touching Tyler's arm. It would be awkward if he became active in the family, but she couldn't let that stop her.

He belonged with the O'Bannons, and she was going to do everything in her power to make sure he stayed.

Of course…that might also be self-serving. Especially if the family kept matchmaking the way they'd been doing. Megan stared at Tyler. She didn't believe anything could happen between them, not for a minute, but something made her touch the ring on the third finger of her left hand. Without giving herself time to think, she slipped it off and dropped it into her pocket.

Removing a wedding ring didn't mean anything, she reasoned. And she felt like a hypocrite wearing the darn thing, considering she'd been ready to file for a divorce when Brad was killed.

Really, it didn't mean a thing.

Chapter Six

"Now pull each string up with your pinkies, then around and catch it with your other fingers," Kara instructed.

"What does it do?" Tyler asked, staring at the string twisted around her hands, a confused expression on his handsome face. A swath of dark hair had fallen forward on his forehead, making him seem younger and less reserved.

"I pull the strings back another way and it makes another shape."

Megan grinned in sympathy. Kara was trying to teach Tyler cat's cradle, but she wasn't the best teacher in the world. The amazing thing was how patient Tyler had been, waiting while she untangled the string each time they messed up, then attempting to work the game again.

By his own admission, Tyler wasn't accustomed to children, but his occasional awkwardness didn't matter to Kara; her daughter was starved for fatherly attention. Megan's grin wavered at the thought and she sighed. It was painfully obvious that Kara was getting her hopes up about something that wasn't going to happen.

"Uh...pinch the string where it crosses," Kara suggested.

For the dozenth time Tyler tried to follow her directions, but one of the loops slipped off his thumb and it was a hopeless tangle once again.

"Sorry," he said, clearly perplexed as to why anyone would play with string in the first place.

"That's okay," Kara assured, patting his shoulder. "It took me a long time, too. But Mom's the best with cat's cradle. She can do lots of tricks."

"Maybe you and your mother could demonstrate for me, then I'd get a better feel for what to do."

Instant panic filled Megan at the suggestion. They'd gotten back from another afternoon of softball at the park, where she hadn't been any more successful avoiding Tyler than she had all morning. But at least with everyone playing softball or sitting in the bleachers watching, they couldn't get into another uncomfortable discussion. If she got down on that quilt where they were sitting...

She cleared her throat. "Well—"

"Come on, Mom," Kara cried before she could get her protest out. "Let's show Tyler."

"Do show him, dear," Eleanor urged. The weather was unusually warm for October and they were sitting under the shade of an awning, enjoying the lazy Friday afternoon. It was the sort of day Megan loved—a time when being with family was more important than anything you did or didn't do.

Avoiding Tyler's knowing gaze, Megan joined her

daughter on the ground. "I've got a longer string," she said, pulling it from a pocket. "It's easier to use when your hands are bigger."

"Are you saying I have big hands?" Tyler whispered close to her ear.

Megan's eyes were inevitably drawn to his long fingers. They were strong, capable hands, calloused on the palms from work, and she had a sudden longing to have him touch her. Tyler's skin wouldn't be cold, but hard and hot and knowing on her body. Heat crawled up her neck, starting from her breasts, and she drew a deep breath.

"Mummy, do you want to start?"

The question brought Megan down to earth in a hurry and she gulped. Lord, how could she be having such torrid thoughts around Tyler? With her daughter not two feet away? She'd completely lost her mind.

"Yes, I'll start." She hurriedly tied the two ends of the string together and looped it over her fingers.

Since Kara was a better student than teacher, they were able to demonstrate the basic cat's cradle moves to Tyler without a misstep. Back and forth between them until the string became tight with twists, and then the more complicated moves backward, to unwind the string.

"That's something," Tyler murmured.

Megan peeked at him from the corner of her eyes, wondering if he was being sarcastic, but he seemed genuinely interested in the child's game and sadness swept through her. Cat's cradle was just one more thing Tyler had missed in his childhood.

No wonder he didn't know how to relate to family or just have fun, he'd never really learned how to play. While she couldn't claim her own childhood as being overwhelmingly happy, she'd had far more than Tyler.

"Show him the witch's broom, Mom."

Smiling, Megan arranged the circle of string over her fingers, then made the moves necessary to create a witch's broom. With a few quick twists of the string she had the "handle" in one hand and the "bristles" in the other. She danced the broom through the air as if brushing up puffs of air.

"Clever," Tyler said lazily. He leaned back on one elbow and watched Megan play with her daughter, thinking he'd rarely seen a more appealing sight. Megan had changed into her jeans for the softball game, then changed back into a dress after returning home from the park. She sat gracefully on the quilt, the skirt flared out around her, her hair caught loosely in a twisted ponytail.

Unlike some natural redheads, she didn't have a single freckle, instead her skin was a delicious cream with warm peach highlights. She even smelled like peaches, as sweet and fresh as the real thing. Of course, there was nothing wrong with freckles, they could be quite appealing. He would have enjoyed counting Megan's freckles, if she'd had any.

"Do Jacob's ladder," Kara said, and Megan deftly created the string masterpiece, followed by the witch's cap and several other string sculptures.

"I had no idea there was so much variety in a game like this," he murmured.

"Now you try it, Tyler," Kara ordered. A warning sound from Megan made her bite her lip. "Uhm...please," she added.

He obeyed, sitting up and trying to duplicate Megan's intricate moves without much success. Not that it was surprising, he'd spent most of the time watching her face, rather than the string.

"Please show him, Mom."

Megan swallowed visibly when Tyler held out his hands. "It appears to be the only way I'm going to learn," he said. "Maybe if you guide my fingers...?"

It was a sneaky trick, but she wasn't going to touch him otherwise, so Tyler gave a mental shrug. He wouldn't burn in hell over an innocent game of cat's cradle, and it *would* be easier to learn if Megan helped.

Fixing her gaze on the string rather than looking into his face, Megan guided his fingers through the moves. She went through three basic sets with him, then settled back on her heel. "You should have it now. Go ahead."

Though he'd gone along with the game to please Kara, a small flush of triumph went through Tyler when he correctly retrieved the string for the first time. It was kind of interesting, the different ways to pull and twist the loops and come up with new, workable patterns.

Together he and Kara worked the string until it became tightly twisted. But when he tried to reverse the process like Megan, he discovered his hands were too large. He simply couldn't get into the small area between Kara's fingers.

"You did real good," Kara said consolingly. She gave him a sunny smile. "Do you want to play badminton now?"

"Uh...I think I'll sit here with your mom for a while."

Kara looked from him to her mother, then back

again, and her smile grew wider. "Okay. I'll see you later, Tyler." She skipped down toward the flat grassy area where a badminton net had been put up earlier.

"I've got some things to do," Megan said as soon as her daughter was out of earshot.

He raised an eyebrow. "That didn't take long."

"Take long for what?"

"For you to run away," he said softly, just loud enough for her to hear, and no one else.

A spark of anger simmered in Megan's green eyes and she crossed her arms over her stomach. "I am *not* running away."

"Seems to me you've been running away all day."

Breath hissed out between her teeth and she glared. "I have responsibilities. I'm busy, that's all." Megan jumped up and marched toward the house.

Tyler sighed and his fingers closed around the tangled circle of string he still held. So much for sitting with Megan and enjoying the sunshine. Most of the time he couldn't just sit like that. There were always things to be done, meetings, papers to go over, plans to consult, but Megan gave him a sense of peace.

"You could go after her," Eleanor suggested.

He turned his head. "I think she wants to be alone."

"Megan is alone too much as it is. Does her good to have a good-looking man pay attention. She..." Eleanor hesitated. "Tell her how beautiful she is, Tyler. Every woman should hear that."

Every woman should hear that.

The back of Tyler's neck prickled, the way it did when he sensed a mystery. He knew practically nothing about the family, or what Megan's life had been with Brad, though it was clear they'd had problems. But he was getting the distinct impression that Megan was uncertain of herself as a woman.

And he remembered his impressions the day before...the changes in Megan. The sweet seduction in her eyes and smile was gone, and in its place was an unexplained pain.

"I think I'll check to see if Megan needs help," he muttered, jumping to his feet. He was aware of Eleanor and the other family members' pleased smiles as he headed for the house, but it didn't matter.

The only thing that mattered was getting some answers.

Megan stared at her pantry shelves without really seeing them. And it was a huge, old-style pantry, something she'd always wanted when she was living with Brad in their modern Los Angeles penthouse. In her opinion, modern homes weren't really built for living, they were built for showing off how much money you had.

In the case of the penthouse, the kitchen hadn't been suitable for making coffee, much less cooking. That was probably because people living in a penthouse were expected to eat at the best restaurants every night, instead of living an ordinary mortal life. Not that she could cook in the beginning of her marriage, she'd just always wanted to.

She'd wanted a lot out of her marriage, just not the things her husband thought were so important.

"You're staring at that shelf like it has writing from heaven on it. Are you getting any answers?"

Somehow, Megan wasn't surprised to hear Tyler's voice; he was the dark cloud of doom hanging over her weekend. Cornering her in the spice-scented pantry was nothing.

"I was thinking about making something."

"Such as?"

"I don't know. A cake, I guess."

"Megan, you have seven cakes sitting in the kitchen right this minute. At the rate you're feeding this crowd they won't be able to walk by Sunday, much less go home."

"Then they can stay. I have room." She wasn't really paying attention to the conversation, just to the way he made her feel...sort of unsettled and safe and terrified, all at the same time. How could one man make her feel such extremes?

"Are you afraid to be alone?"

She blinked. Afraid to be alone? What a ridiculous notion. "What are you talking about?"

"You just said..." Tyler stopped, frowning. "You said everyone could stay."

"Of course. Family is always welcome, but that doesn't mean I'm afraid to be alone. There are worse things than being alone," she muttered.

From the expression on Tyler's face she could see he didn't understand. How could he? Tyler had confidence to spare; he didn't know what it was like to hate looking at yourself in a mirror, wondering what you lacked. He certainly didn't know what it was like to have your husband cut you down with a single disparaging look or comment.

"Do you miss Brad, is that the problem? I thought you said the marriage was a mistake."

"*No*. I don't miss him." Even as the denial left

her mouth, Megan regretted it. The two men hadn't gotten along that well, but that didn't mean Tyler would appreciate hearing she didn't miss his cousin. "Look, this has nothing to do with Brad. I'm just concerned about the reunion being a success, that's all."

"I'm no expert, but I don't see why it's all your responsibility. I can't imagine the O'Bannons expecting you to take it all on yourself."

Megan's feet stirred restlessly. The pantry seemed so small with Tyler standing in the door, small and intimate. And the air was warmer than it ought to be, though her hormones were probably responsible for any temperature problems. She smoothed her fingers over the skirt of her dress.

"They don't expect anything. Your family is wonderful, Tyler. They've done so much for me and Kara, I naturally want to do something in return. Remember when we talked about the house…?"

He nodded. "Yes, but I don't see what that has to do with the reunion."

She tried to look somewhere besides Tyler's face, which left focusing on the rest of his body, which wasn't soothing in the least. "You have no idea how hard they worked, helping me put this place back together. I'm sure they all thought I was nuts buying such a wrecked-out house, but they never said anything. They just pitched in. Having the reunion here is a way of saying how much I appreciate it."

"I doubt they thought you were nuts."

"You didn't see what it looked like before we started," she said dryly.

Tyler wished that he *had* been there, helping right along with everyone else. But he couldn't have handled seeing Megan and wondering how much she was grieving for another man. Now…he didn't know what to think. She'd said her marriage was a mistake, but that didn't mean she'd loved Brad any less.

"I've seen plenty of trashed buildings," he said. "That doesn't mean they don't have potential. And you were right about this house, it's great. I'm glad you saved it."

Her smile took his breath away. "The county was planning to condemn the place when I put an offer down."

"Then you did the right thing."

"Thanks."

Tyler waited, then asked something that had been bothering him the day before. "Megan, I don't understand why you started the bed and breakfast inn. Don't you have enough money without working so hard?"

The bright smile on her face vanished. "We're okay."

"That doesn't answer my question."

Megan moved restlessly, but he stood his ground at the door. She'd have to push past him to get out, and before that happened he wanted some answers.

"Brad wasn't…good with money," she said reluctantly. "But I have an inheritance from my maternal grandparents and I've been successful writing children's books, so Kara and I are fine."

"What about the bed and breakfast inn?"

"I only take tourists during the summer." She wrinkled her nose. "Mostly overflow guests from Grady and Eleanor's B&B. They insist on doing the bookings for both of us—that way they make sure I get customers they've known forever. They're a little protective.''

"Good.'' Tyler felt a measure of relief at the news. He hadn't liked the idea of Megan opening her doors to strangers. ''You don't take anybody late at night, do you?''

"Not that it's any of your concern, but no I don't.''

"Keep it that way. You let Grady and Eleanor handle the bookings,'' he ordered. ''Don't take anyone they haven't vetted first.''

Megan looked at him narrowly and tapped her foot. ''I'll handle my bookings the way I want to handle them. You don't have any say in this.''

"You're a woman alone, you have to be more careful.''

All at once the irritation in Megan's face vanished and she sighed. ''That's word for word what Grady keeps saying. He sent you in here, didn't he? Or Eleanor did. Tell them they don't have to worry, I'm always cautious. If I expand it'll be through a regular tour guide agency.''

"Isn't it possible that I'm concerned on my own?'' Tyler demanded. ''That I might be worried about you?''

"You hardly know me.''

A growling sound he didn't recognize came from his throat. Lord, Megan could drive a sane man absolutely bonkers, though sexual frustration was making him the craziest. ''That isn't true.''

"You don't have to be nice to me because of Grady and Eleanor,'' Megan pointed out in a reasonable tone. ''I know Grams is matchmaking, but she'll get over it.''

"This has nothing to do with Eleanor."

"Of course it does."

The worst part about Megan's statement was that she actually seemed to believe it. Yet Tyler had seen flashes of awareness in her green eyes, subtle acknowledgement that she was a woman and he was a man, and that there were interesting biological differences between the two of them. She *must* have seen the same interest in him.

Hadn't she?

"I care about you," Tyler said, trying to sound calm. "Of course I'm concerned about Eleanor, but that has nothing to do with the two of us."

"There isn't 'the two of us.' There's me, and there's you. So, if that's all, I'd better get started." Megan blindly grabbed a box from the opposite shelf and tried to slide past Tyler.

"I don't think that'll make a very good cake," he drawled, his arm shooting out to block her exit.

Chagrined, Megan looked down at the box of Italian seasoned bread crumbs she was clutching. What was it about Tyler that made her do such foolish things? It was annoying. After nine years she was just as susceptible as ever.

"Maybe I'll make a meatloaf."

"Maybe you should put the box down and talk to me."

"We talked."

"Okay. I can think of more pleasurable things to do." His already low voice had dropped another octave, reminding Megan of distant thunder.

"I don't know what…" Her protest trailed as she looked up and saw the intense gleam in Tyler's eyes. Swallowing, Megan backed up until she bumped into the opposite wall. She dropped the box of bread-crumbs, missing the shelf by inches.

He walked forward, casually kicking the door closed behind him.

"T-Tyler? What are you doing?"

"I'm doing something I wanted to do nine years ago. And since you didn't realize it back then, I want to be sure you don't miss it now."

Megan's heart seemed to stop, then raced ahead at twice its normal rate. She hadn't felt so excited and scared since she was sixteen and about to be kissed for the first time.

Tyler reached down and retrieved the dropped box, setting it properly on the shelf. "Wouldn't want to step on this, would we?"

"Er...no."

His finger traced her temple, down her cheek, and settled in the fluttering hollow of her throat.

Knowing she was in danger of hyperventilating, Megan tried to slow her breathing. Tyler would stop if she said so...she just didn't want him to stop. She'd wanted to kiss him from the moment they'd met, and had felt guilty about it ever since. But there was nothing to feel guilty about now. Neither one of them had any commitments.

Even the knowledge that she might disappoint him couldn't calm the way her pulse was racing.

"Megan...you're so amazing," Tyler breathed.

"No, I'm not."

"Shhh. Don't argue."

Megan didn't want to argue, she just wanted to *feel*...Tyler's mouth, his hands, every part of him. He was a fantasy, hidden deep within her soul, so deeply she'd hardly known he was there, except for the vague stirrings of guilt that came with his name. She lifted her hand, tempted by the warm width of Tyler's chest.

If you couldn't please your husband, what hope do you have with Tyler?

The reminder drilled into Megan's consciousness like a corrosive acid and she flinched.

"It's no good," she said. "I can't."

Tyler didn't step away, he simply smiled. "Can't what?" he murmured. "Kiss me? It's very simple. Just lean a little this way and open your mouth." He pulled her closer. "You have such a beautiful mouth."

"No."

Tyler saw the denial in her green eyes. The unwillingness to believe the smallest compliment.

Brad, what the hell did you do to her? he thought furiously. But there wasn't an answer. Ghosts didn't answer for their sins, they just stayed, wreaking their damage on the living and refusing to leave.

Tyler tugged Megan into the wide stance between his legs, silently urging her to relax. "You smell so good. Sweet, like summer peaches."

"It's my shampoo."

A chuckle rumbled from his chest. The response was prosaic, but her voice was hoarse and damned sexy. "In that case, don't ever change shampoos."

But he'd waited so long, he couldn't wait any longer. With a sigh of relief Tyler caught her mouth with his own, his hand sliding down her back and arching her body upward. The soft imprint of Megan's breasts burned into him, searing away coherent thought.

"Tyler," she moaned, his name muffled, lost in the hungry kiss.

Exhilaration and fear raced through Megan at a dead heat. Finally, *finally* she knew what it was like to have Tyler's arms around her, their breath mingling together, his hands touching her with sure, knowing strength.

But the fear was still there. Fear of caustic words. Of disappointment. Of Tyler realizing she was less than he needed.

Less.

Not enough...never enough for a man like Tyler.

Nausea rose in her stomach, displacing everything else. She stiffened without intending to.

"It's all right," Tyler said softly. "Don't think."

Megan clung to his shoulders, trying to focus on the sensations cascading through her body. Tyler's mouth, hot and open over hers, his tongue moving like rough velvet over her teeth, his hands clasping her waist. And pressed to her abdomen, the urgent swell of his arousal.

Slowly she rubbed against him, savoring the evidence that she pleased him in some way.

"You're making me crazy, Megan."

Uncertain, Megan hesitated.

"No...don't stop. Please don't stop," he groaned, urging her impossibly closer, kissing his way down her neck.

Too drunk with sensation now to think, she swayed again, her hands easing upward. His hair was like crisp silk, cool beneath her fingertips, and she dreamily compared its softness to Tyler's hard length.

She arched backward as he kissed his way to the

first swell of her breasts. The thought of him touching her so intimately sent shudders through Megan, her nipples tightening with a sensual ache.

"Say yes, honey."

"Yes," she replied, though she couldn't imagine what he was asking, much less care.

Cool air against her skin was the first clue she might have said yes to something she was unprepared to handle, and Megan's eyes shot open as she realized he'd unbuttoned the pearl buttons on her bodice. His fingers deftly released the front clasp of bra, gently caressing the curve of her breast in the process.

"I mean, *no*," she gasped.

Megan shimmied a scant three inches away, pressing into the corner where the pantry shelves met. She clutched the sweetheart neck of her dress together and stared into Tyler's turbulent eyes.

"I shouldn't...have said yes."

"Why not?"

Because I don't want you to look at me, that's why, Megan thought mutinously. It would be different if it was dark and he couldn't really see, but the bare light bulb hanging from the ceiling would reveal every detail of her not-so-perfect body.

"Honey?"

"Cut it out. I'm not your honey."

"You taste like honey," Tyler said. He put one arm out and leaned against the pantry shelf, his hair tousled from her fingers. "Wild honey. I want to taste it...everywhere." His gaze slid down her, as tangible as a caress.

"Tyler, don't," Megan pleaded, her knees shaking. She wanted him, and it was tearing her apart.

Even if things were different, she couldn't have a casual affair with him. She was a mother and widow, living in a small town. Times changed, but they didn't change that much. Not for her, not when loving Tyler promised both heaven and hell.

"Let me see you," he whispered. "For nine years I've dreamed of kissing you...tasting you."

Shivering, wondering how she could survive if she saw disappointment in Tyler's face, Megan closed her eyes and stuffed her hands behind her back. She was twenty-seven years old and acting like a naive virgin. It wasn't as if a man had never looked at her before.

Breathing a sigh of relief that he hadn't scared her off completely, Tyler brushed his lips against Megan's forehead. Slowly he poured kisses on her face, memorizing each fraction of satin skin.

The tension gripping her body eased and her arms crept about his waist in a small measure of trust, so fragile he was afraid to move for fear of crushing it.

He shouldn't have pushed, Tyler realized. Whatever demons Megan was fighting, she needed someone patient, someone who would give her time. He was too rough, too hard and too damned *hungry*. He'd gotten an education, of sorts, while serving in the military, but it didn't amount to much.

But none of it mattered when Megan leaned into him a moment later.

"I could spend the next hundred years just kissing you," he murmured against her throat. "Want to sneak out tonight? Friday is date night, after all. We could park in my car and neck. I never got to do that when I was a teenager."

"Me...either."

"I'll even keep my hands to myself," he promised.

The kind of innocent kissing Tyler was offering made Megan ache with longing. He made an art of kissing, slow and sweet, as if there was all the time in the world. And though she'd given him permission to touch her more intimately, his hands were conspicuously absent from the area below her collar bones.

Why? Had he realized that after having a baby and nursing her for eight months, she wasn't a nubile eighteen any longer?

A flicker of the feminine pride her husband hadn't quite been able to kill rose to the surface. "We're going to be missed," she said.

"We have time."

"No, we..." Megan's thoughts scattered as Tyler brushed across her breast with the back of his hand.

"Lots and lots of time," he assured, teasing her nipple into a tight, hard bud. Suddenly it no longer mattered about the revealing light bulb overhead, all that mattered was the way he held her, touching her, drinking her in.

The muscles in Megan's abdomen clenched and released as Tyler circled each of her breasts in turn, teasing the throbbing tip with only the heat of his breath.

She moaned, her head falling back.

After an endless wait he drew her into the warmth of his mouth, suckling one nipple while his fingers both soothed and excited the other.

A tingling warmth unraveled through her body, unlike anything she'd ever felt before. The thought went through her mind that she wanted to stay like this forever…floating, shivering, her blood pouring like champagne bubbles through her veins.

But the sensation changed, the tingle turning into an unbearable need for something just beyond her reach.

Tyler's free hand cupped her bottom, lifting her, increasing the intimate alignment with his body. She could feel his need, pressing at the juncture of her thighs, and it took all her will to keep from wrapping her legs around his hips.

Distantly, through the rush of blood in her ears, came the sound of doors slamming. Of talking and laughter and youthful questions.

"Tyler?"

"What?" The tip of his tongue drew a damp trail to her other breast. "Much, *much* better than honey," he muttered, shaping her with his mouth and teeth.

"Th-things are breaking up outside."

"Mmmm…yeah. Must be getting chilly with the sun going down." Tyler shifted, setting her on the wide work counter that extended the length of the pantry, leaving both his hands free for sensual exploration.

Megan closed her eyes, clinging to the stolen moment. Her fingers clenched on the worn, satin-smooth patina of the wood counter.

"Mo-o-om!" called a voice. "Where are you?"

She gulped, realizing it was Kara. Her daughter could have walked in on them…kissing.

His chest heaving, Tyler jerked away. He rested against the wall, hands gathered into fists and resting on his thighs. "Sorry," he muttered.

Sorry?

Megan shuddered. She had enough regrets of her

own without dealing with his. "Apology accepted. It won't happen again, though I have to point out that you started this particular scene."

Tyler measured the brittle chill in Megan's voice and shook his head. "Honey, I'm just sorry about the timing. Everything else was perfect."

Chapter Seven

Everything else was perfect.

Megan fastened her bra and the buttons on her dress, her face burning under Tyler's gaze. He did seem to approve of the way she looked, judging by the rigid tension of his muscles. And he still seemed...eager.

She hastily averted her eyes from the bulging zipper on his jeans.

"Men can't hide what they feel," he said calmly, accepting biological reality without a trace of embarrassment. "Which can be damned inconvenient at times like this."

"I'll go out and...uh...you know."

"Give me a minute?"

"Right."

"Good idea."

Tyler stifled a groan when Megan slipped through the pantry door. He was so aroused it hurt to breathe, much less move. She was every bit as sweet and hot as he'd dreamed. Whatever had happened to make her uncertain as a woman, it hadn't destroyed her ability to respond. She was so responsive he'd forgotten everything but her soft moans and the way she tasted.

But despite the way Megan had returned his kisses, he knew he'd pushed too hard and too fast.

It was a few minutes before Tyler could bring his body under control. Taking deep breaths, he concentrated on the fragrance in the pantry, a mixture of spice and apples and molasses...and the lingering scent of peaches.

"Oh, yeah. That's going to work," he growled, remembering how the elusive hint of peaches followed Megan. But then, everything in the big old Victorian mansion was going to remind him of her, so it probably didn't matter.

Finally able to straighten without too much pain, Tyler ran his fingers through his hair. The pantry opened onto a large utility porch and he paused there another moment, listening to the bustle of people in the rest of the house.

For all of Megan's disquiet around him—for reasons he was only beginning to understand—she was doing her darndest to make him comfortable with the family. He thought about it for a minute, looking into the kitchen, which was alive with female O'Bannons.

Megan had taken tray after tray of lasagna from her enormous chest freezer. *Homemade* lasagna. If the rest of her cooking was any indication, he'd be in Italian heaven by supper time. The women were happily preparing a green salad and slicing French bread for heating in the oven.

As if aware of his scrutiny, Megan looked up, her

cheeks flushing when she locked gazes with him. Tyler grinned lazily, but the private moment passed when Toni Carter caught sight of him and motioned vigorously for him to come inside.

He just hoped everyone didn't realize he'd been holed-up inside Megan's pantry, wishing she was still there with him, and that the rest of his family was in some other state.

It wouldn't be polite.

Megan was quiet during dinner, preoccupied with thoughts of Tyler. He was making her crazy. Here she was, Brad's widow, and she'd practically made love with Tyler in the middle of the O'Bannon reunion.

And what bothered her most was that she didn't feel guilty about it. Well, not *that* guilty. Of course, the O'Bannons were in the happily-ever-after cheering section, so it probably didn't mean anything.

Happily ever after…the classic fairy-tale ending.

She knew better than anyone that there wasn't any such thing. Life wasn't that clean and neat. It might work for some people, but not for her.

"Megan, your lasagna is wonderful," Toni said as she took a bite. "I wish I could cook like this, but I'm a dead loss in the kitchen. Just ask Jack. The second time he needed his stomach pumped he said, 'Honey, if we ever get married, let's hire someone to do the cooking.'"

Jack forked a mouthful of pasta into his mouth and munched it down. "I didn't need my stomach pumped, I just drank some Alka Seltzer and everything was okay. I was nervous," he said confidingly.

"I had an engagement ring in my pocket, but I was sure she'd say 'no.'"

Megan forced a smile to her lips. "Toni, with your figure, you don't have to cook."

The other woman patted her expanded stomach. "You mean, my figure with this little bundle on the way?"

"I mean *any*time. If you weren't so nice, I'd be terribly jealous. You make pregnancy beautiful."

"I think your figure is just fine, Megan," Tyler said.

He sat across the table and whenever she looked up, he was watching her. Knowing exactly how *much* of her figure he'd seen sent heat zigzagging through her tummy.

She averted her gaze. From the grinning faces around the table, she was certain that everyone had guessed something had happened between her and Tyler.

The mangled lasagna on her own plate didn't look appealing, but Megan pushed it around with her fork, hoping nobody would notice she wasn't eating. Nobody except Tyler, that is. He seemed to notice everything.

With so much family attending the reunion they were spread throughout the downstairs, tables set up in every convenient corner. They'd borrowed the tables and chairs from the church and would return them Sunday afternoon.

After Tyler left.

Megan's fork grated on her plate. Everything reminded her of him. She didn't know how to handle the way he made her feel. Passion wasn't something she knew anything about. She wasn't good at sex—

she'd barely started getting tingles by the time Brad was rolling over and saying goodnight.

But Tyler...he was overwhelming. He might have some small interest in her for the weekend, but she could never satisfy him in the long term.

Any remaining appetite she might have had vanished with the thought. Her husband had hurt her terribly with his cheating and unkindness, but Tyler could destroy her. It was something she knew with absolute certainty, an understanding that came from a deep, instinctive level.

"Is there any more garlic bread?" asked Jack Carter. He shook the empty bread basket with a mournful expression.

"Yes, in the kitchen." Megan quickly pushed her chair back and got to her feet.

"You stay right there, Megan. Go get it yourself," Toni instructed her husband.

"No, I'll go." Megan retrieved the basket from Jack, then hurried into the kitchen and drew a long breath.

If it wasn't for Tyler, she'd be having a great time. Normally she loved gatherings with the O'Bannons. They were the family she'd always wanted, and they'd made a place for her in their hearts that was more precious than gold.

"Thought you might need help."

Startled, Megan dropped an entire loaf of bread on the floor. She should have guessed Tyler would follow her, so she should have been prepared.

"I don't need help with garlic bread. It weighs about ten ounces," she muttered. Kneeling, she collected the scattered slices and tossed them in the garbage can. "You should wear a bell," she added for good measure. "Something to warn people that you're sneaking up on them."

"I wasn't sneaking."

"Okay, fine. Have it your way." Megan sighed. She'd known inviting Tyler to the reunion would complicate things, she just hadn't known how much.

Kara had a crush on Tyler that wouldn't quit, and now she was angling for a new father with all the subtlety of a bulldozer. The family wasn't being much more subtle about the matter, and then *she'd* gone and kissed him in the pantry. She'd never be able to walk into the pantry again without her knees getting wobbly.

Tyler casually filled the bread basket, though his eyes remained fixed on Megan. "We have to talk."

"No."

"Hon—"

"No." With short, jerky movements she washed her hands at the sink. "No honeys, no kisses, no nothing," she continued in a quieter tone. "We shouldn't have started anything in the first place, because it won't be going anywhere."

"How do you know that?"

"Because it won't. There's no such thing as a happy ending, Tyler. Not for some people."

Tyler sighed. Megan could erect walls faster than any women he'd ever known. He'd have to find a way of breaking them down again.

"Okay, let's talk about Eleanor," he said, knowing it was the one subject Megan wouldn't reject.

She turned. "What about Eleanor?"

"Wait...I'm going to take the bread out first so Jack doesn't come looking for it." Tyler went through the swinging door, set the basket on the table, then strode back into the kitchen. He found Megan sitting at the breakfast table, rubbing her temples.

"Another headache?" he asked, dropping in the chair across from her.

She slanted a look at him. "Something like that."

Tyler really wanted to discuss the two of them, but he wouldn't get far under the circumstances. And he couldn't blame Megan. They were a long way from resolving anything between them. Kissing had just complicated things, and things were already pretty complicated.

"About Eleanor...does she always eat that way?"

"You mean doesn't eat," Megan said flatly. "Mostly it's just toast and tea, like I said this morning. Dry toast, for that matter."

"Is she ever in pain?"

"Sometimes—in her back and right side. But she won't really talk about it. The only thing she says is that you have to expect some aches and pains when you get old."

Tyler tapped his fingers on the table. "That's a cro—" He stopped and grinned sheepishly. "I mean, that's nonsense. A friend of mine is a doctor who specializes in elder care. He's always saying that people don't have to be uncomfortable in their latter years. Besides, we're a long-lived family, so Eleanor and Grady really aren't that old."

Besides, we're a long-lived family....

We're.

It was the first time Megan had ever heard Tyler talk about the O'Bannons as *his* family. They were always "the" family, or "not really family." Warmth crept around her heart, buoying it, making her feel better even though she was still worried about Eleanor and that kiss.

And really, she shouldn't worry about the kiss so much. Big deal. It was a kiss. Tyler liked to kiss, and she hadn't been entirely uncooperative. She could dismiss the part about him having wanted to kiss her for nine years. He was a man. What else would he say?

"Anyway," Tyler continued, oblivious to her internal dialogue. "This thing with Eleanor is really bothering me, so I called my friend before dinner. He had a bunch of questions that I couldn't answer. I thought you might be able to help fill in the blanks."

Megan frowned. "You can't diagnose an illness long distance."

"No, but there are things we can look for, then use it to prod Eleanor into seeing a doctor."

"What do you think we've been trying to do?" Megan asked, irritated. "That's what we've all been—"

"I know, I know," Tyler said quickly. He shrugged and a guilty expression spread across his face. "Actually, he isn't on call this weekend, so I asked him to drive up tomorrow and check her out. He'll order any tests he thinks are necessary, and next week we'll take her to San Francisco to have them."

Megan bit her lip. It was direct. Immediate. And totally Tyler. And because it was Tyler, he was possibly the only member of the family who could get away with it.

"Eleanor isn't going to like that."

"Too bad. If she'd just see a doctor, we wouldn't have to go to these lengths."

"I don't think she's going to buy that reasoning, either. Would you?"

"Probably not."

They sat for another minute in a comfortable silence, then Tyler got up, poured them each a cup of coffee, and sat down again.

"They're nice people," he said quietly. "The nicest I've ever met. Thing is…I knew it when I was a rebellious teenager, but I was so damned stubborn about everything."

"I see." Megan had to laugh. "And of course you've changed and aren't like that anymore."

He chuckled. "No, I'm still stubborn."

"Grady said they wanted to put you through college, but you refused and enlisted in the army instead."

"Yeah." Tyler sipped his coffee, his eyes distant with memories. "It felt like it was charity, and I was sick to death of charity. That's all I heard when I was growing up, about how the government was taking care of me and how grateful I ought to be for that damned group home."

"You were a child. It wasn't fair for them to talk like that," Megan said indignantly.

"I don't think anyone was concerned about being fair at the home, they were just hoping for survival. The day a kid turned eighteen, their bed was assigned to someone else," he said, remembering. "That was it. One day you had a place to sleep, the next you didn't."

Tyler focused on the blue gingham fabric of the tablecloth. It went nicely with the vase of white and yellow daisies and the cobalt glass salt and pepper shakers that Megan had put out earlier. She did everything nicely.

At the group home he'd worked his share of chores in the institutional kitchen, helping serve food and wash dishes. He'd hated that big fluorescent-lit room with its stainless steel ovens and refrigerators and counters. Megan's kitchen wasn't like that. Out of necessity she had commercial-grade equipment because of the bed and breakfast business, but it still felt like a real home, with all the little touches that made the difference.

"Tyler...."

"Don't look so sad," he murmured. He hated seeing sorrow in Megan's green eyes, she was made for smiles, not tears. "I was living with Grady and Eleanor by the time I turned eighteen, remember?"

"But you enlisted on your eighteenth birthday. Surely you didn't think they'd throw you out...did you?"

Tyler looked at her in shock. "Of course not. Even when I was eighteen I was smarter than that. They were great to me—it wasn't their fault I couldn't appreciate it. Hell, I shouldn't have told you that stuff. I've never told anyone what it was like at the home."

"I'm glad you did." A burst of laughter from the dining made Megan jump. "I guess we should go back out and join the family."

"Why? You weren't eating, you were just moving food around on your plate."

"Because it's a time to enjoy each other," she said gently.

"I'm enjoying you right now."

"Oh." Megan's eyelids swept down, yet not before Tyler saw the pleasure his comment had given her.

Somewhere between the pantry and his first bite of lasagna, he'd realized he couldn't back away from her, not this time. He had to understand his feelings for Megan. He couldn't spend the next nine years wondering what might have happened if he'd stayed.

But it wouldn't be easy.

She was every bit as stubborn as he was, though she'd never admit it.

The faint swoosh of a door opening turned both their heads and they saw a sheepish Jack, holding out an empty lasagna pan. "Sorry to interrupt anything, but I figured there was more food out here."

"There's plenty," Megan said. She slid out of her chair and took the empty casserole from Jack, motioning with her elbow to the foil-covered pans on the stove. "They've been out of the oven for a while so I don't think you need a hot pad—but it should still be good and warm."

"Great." Jack took one of the pans, pausing to give Tyler a broad wink before going back into the dining room.

A wink Megan saw.

"What's that about?" she demanded. It was one thing for her to get cozy with Tyler in the pantry, another for him to be telling someone else about it.

"What's what about?"

"That wink Jack just gave you."

"Nothing."

Because she was close to the door into the dining room and she didn't want anybody to hear, Megan clenched her teeth together until she got back to the breakfast nook. "That wasn't 'nothing,'" she insisted. "That was the kind of wink men give to each other when they're…they're being *men*."

"Of course we're men," Tyler said, looking bewildered.

"Did you tell him about…that." She threw her hand up to her shoulder, thumb pointing toward the pantry.

"No." Tyler now looked appalled, which wasn't any improvement over bewildered. "Teenage boys brag about things like that, grown men have more respect for their partners."

Some of the steam escaped Megan. As usual she'd overreacted, but she wasn't handling Tyler very well.

"So what was Jack doing?" she asked more reasonably. "He winked for some reason."

"I don't know. Hey, you tell me. You know him better than I do."

Megan opened her mouth, then shut it again. Normally when Tyler said something like that he was trying to distance himself from the family, but this time it sounded reasonable. He was right, she did know Jack better. Jack was a good guy. A little on the boisterous side, but he was right for Toni, and that was all that really mattered.

"Let it go," Tyler said, taking her hand and tugging her toward the chair she'd vacated two minutes before. "Along with everyone else, Jack has been hinting that I get together with you. I'm sure it hasn't escaped the family's notice that we've been absent from the table for over ten minutes, so he was probably trying to offer some encouragement."

"You mean matchmaking."

A smile played across Tyler's lips. "Right. You don't want to deprive them of their fun, do you?"

Megan liked that smile, it was warm and fuzzy and his eyes smiled just as much as the rest of him. If anyone could convince Eleanor to see a doctor, then Tyler could. Heck, he could talk a woman into practically anything.

"Maybe, maybe not. But if you're not careful," she said, getting up and walking to the stove. "You could find yourself married by Sunday. That wouldn't be good for such a dedicated bachelor."

Tyler watched as Megan lifted one of the pans of lasagna and headed for the dining-room door. When the door closed behind her, he let out a breath he wasn't aware he'd been holding.

"I'm not as dedicated as you think," he murmured. "Not by a long shot."

After the meal Megan found herself sitting on the couch, her feet resting on the coffee table, and wondering how she'd been talked into sitting down when everybody else was cleaning up. It was her kitchen, she ought to be working instead of being lazy.

It was all Tyler's fault.

He might have charmed her with that killer smile, but she was still willing to blame anything on him that he was willing to take the blame for. *Lord*, that sounds stupid, Megan thought in disgust.

She had a problem with Tyler and she didn't know how to handle it. The problem was the way her pulse reacted around him...not to mention her brain. Every shred of good sense she possessed went flying out the window when he walked into the room. That wasn't good.

Actually, it *was* Tyler who'd insisted she sit down, saying "they" would take care of everything. Megan put her feet back on the floor and restlessly wiggled her toes.

"Relax," Eleanor scolded, settling next to her on the couch. "You've hardly had a moment's rest all day."

"That isn't true, and you know it."

"Perhaps, but you don't have to do everything, my dear."

Megan shrugged. From the beginning of her marriage she'd fallen into a habit of rushing about, trying to be useful at the family gatherings. Being "useful" was the only thing that made her own parents notice her, so it was a pattern she'd developed early in life. But she didn't mind with the O'Bannons, because they never took the things she did for granted.

"I enjoy it," she said sincerely.

"I know, but you've gone overboard with this re-union." Eleanor fixed her with a stern eye. "So loosen up, child."

"Good advice," Tyler said as he walked into the room.

"Of course it's good advice. I'm an old and wise woman."

"I'll agree with the wise part." He bent and gave her a kiss. "But old? Never."

Megan smiled faintly. Tyler was the one who'd needed loosening up, and he was beginning to do exactly that. Families weren't the mystery he thought they were; they were like friends, only better.

"So, what games are we playing tonight?" Eleanor asked, still looking pleased.

"Twister!" Kara exclaimed.

A small niggle of alarm went through Megan.

Twister was a very physical game. She'd already gotten physical enough with Tyler for one day.

"I don't think so, Kara. Grandma can't play Twister."

"Don't worry about me," Eleanor said immediately. "I'll have fun watching."

Tyler looked from Megan to Kara. "What's Twister?"

The youngster brightened. "It's loads of fun. I'll go get it." She dashed out of the room while Megan looked at Tyler with a perplexed frown.

"You've never played Twister?"

"Nope."

Megan would have said something about the game being popular when they were children, but she stopped herself in time. He wasn't familiar with games like Twister because of the way he'd been raised. She was so mad at that group home she wanted to spit, but she didn't saying anything because Tyler had already said he didn't usually talk about the place.

"Here it is," Kara cried. She held the battered box in the air. "Let's play with teams. Reece and Jessie already said they'd play."

"Okay," Megan agreed, seeing a way out. "How about you and Tyler as one team, with Reece and Jessie as the other?"

"Naw. You and Tyler go first against Reece and Jessie. I'll spin."

This definitely wasn't her daughter. Kara was a doer. She jumped in with both feet. There wasn't a game in the house she didn't love, from Bingo to Wild Jacks.

"Sounds good to me," Tyler said. He held out a

hand to Megan, laughter brimming in his eyes. Pulling her upright, he put a hand in the small of her back, urging to the center of the carpet where Kara was spreading out the game sheet.

Megan stared at the rectangular plastic mat, all six by four feet of it. That wasn't very big for four adults, which meant those four adults were going to get very friendly during the game. Her fingers closed around the skirt of her dress.

"You know, I don't think I can play in this dress. Why don't I do the spinning, Kara? That way you can partner with Tyler."

Kara gave her a funny look. "You always say you're more comfortable in a dress, Mom. But it's okay, we can wait while you put on something else."

"Strike three," Tyler whispered in Megan's ear. "Besides, how much trouble can we get into with everyone watching?"

How much trouble?

Megan shivered and headed for the front staircase. She didn't know, but she was sure she was going to find out.

Chapter Eight

Tyler looked down at the heavy white plastic mat
on the floor. It looked innocent enough, but based on
Megan's alarm at the idea of playing with him, he
figured it might be worth pursuing.

Rows of large blue, yellow, green and red circles
marched down the mat. Kara held a cardboard spinner, and from the picture on the box it looked like
players had to put a hand or foot down based on
where the spinner landed.

When Megan returned she was wearing a pair of
black denims and a soft green sweater that clung to
her curves. Tyler whistled silently.

"All right," Eleanor said. She held a sheet of rules
in her hands, reading them from over the top of her
glasses. "Teams stand at opposite sides of the mat,
with their feet on the end circles. Kara will spin and
tell you which hand or foot to move, and to where."

Tyler grinned at Reece, opposite him on the mat.
Reece's fiancée, an attractive blonde, stood next to

him. She played with the engagement ring on her finger, twisting it back and forth until Reece put his hand over hers and squeezed gently.

It was a moment Tyler envied—most of the time Megan did everything possible to avoid contact with him and stiffened when he did touch her. On the other hand, it reminded him that Megan's wedding ring had disappeared, which was a definite step in the right direction.

"Let's see," Eleanor continued. "Team members can cover the same circle with one hand or foot each, but opposing players have to find their own circle."

Ahhhhh. Tyler suddenly understood Megan's reluctance to play. There were unparalleled opportunities for physical contact in a game like this. They could get cozy in relatively innocent circumstances, which meant he would have a chance to break down those barriers she kept putting up. She couldn't ignore him if they were tangled up together.

Good going, Kara, he said silently, sending the child an approving smile.

"That's it," Eleanor said, after citing the remaining rules. She set the instruction sheet down on her lap. "Except the first player that puts a knee or elbow to the mat, or falls, causes their team to lose."

Tyler lifted Megan's left hand and placed a kiss on the soft inner skin of her wrist. "For luck," he whispered.

Megan snatched her arm away, then looked around to see if anybody had noticed. Tyler was impossible. Yet deep inside she felt a shivery anticipation.

She'd played Twister as a kid and with her daughter, but she wasn't a kid any longer and Tyler was all male. No wonder this game had been so popular at junior-high-school parties when she was young. You could get up close and personal without *looking* like you wanted to get personal.

Kara made the first spin. "Tyler, left foot on red."

With a grin only Megan could see, Tyler turned and put his left foot on the closest red circle, straddling the game mat. No matter where her first spin sent her, she'd be all over...or under him. "That's bad strategy," she muttered.

"Oh?"

"You should move into the opponent's territory," she said through her teeth. "Make *them* go under or over you."

"I'll keep that in mind."

Jessie got her spin and shifted her right foot to a yellow spot in the middle of the mat.

"Mom, left hand on blue."

Megan bit the inside of her lip as she glanced down Tyler's body. Putting her left hand on a blue circle was going to put her head and shoulders into intimate proximity with his...thighs. And the worst part was Tyler's grin that said he knew exactly where she'd end up.

Crouching into as tight a ball as possible and keeping her eyes fixed to the mat, Megan extended her left hand, touching two fingers to the closest free blue circle.

He leaned over her, whispering in her ear. "What about strategy? You could have put that hand further into our opponent's territory."

"Don't tempt me," Megan growled back. "You might be sorry."

"Promises, promises."

She gritted her teeth and waited for the next move, hoping it would move him further away.

It didn't.

The next several rounds landed Megan into a twist between the two men. Reece's fiancée proved surprisingly agile as she inched her left foot into the one remaining green circle on the mat. So far she'd escaped some of the absurd gyrations the rest of them had been put to. Megan bit her lip, hoping they didn't look as ridiculous as she felt.

Honestly, the lengths people went to please their children. Kara was the one who'd suggested the game, but was she playing?

No.

Kara was the spinner, sharing referee responsibilities with her great-grandmother.

"Mom, left hand on yellow."

"Oh, goody." Megan lifted her chin and glanced toward the line of yellow circles. She could pretend to slip, losing the game for her team, but she knew Kara would be disappointed.

There were two free yellow circles, but only one was possible as a target. To get there she would have to reach around Tyler's stomach, leaning backward over his leg—virtually wrapping herself around him. Tyler grinned as he caught her eye, obviously understanding her dilemma and enjoying every minute.

Megan shifted slowly. Her one advantage was that Kara still hadn't called a circle for her right hand, which meant she was free to put it anywhere she wanted.

At the moment she wanted to put it around Tyler's throat.

Her body was too sensitized to him, weakening

her resolve to avoid him. Each move of the game had made it worse until she was ready to scream, or attack him or both. And the rat was grinning like a victorious baboon, so he had to know what it was doing to her. For that matter, he'd probably planned the whole thing.

Inching into position, Megan sucked in her breath, trying not to move too much against Tyler. His thigh was rock-hard beneath her, which was a good thing because he was having to support most of her weight.

She reminded herself that there was nothing sexual about a dumb kid's game, especially with everyone watching.

Nothing at all.

Kara sang off another move and Reece lifted his hand, moving it somewhere out of Megan's sight. All at once Jessie yelped and gave him a shove that sent the four of them toppling to the floor.

Though Tyler hadn't expected the sudden loss of balance, he clutched Megan to his chest and rolled so she ended on top. A chuckle started low in his belly and grew until he was laughing out loud. He couldn't believe how much fun he was having. Of course, he was also hotter than El Paso in July, but it just made the laughter sweeter.

Twister must have been designed by a master jokester, who knew precisely what his game would do to the players. Tyler lifted his head, looking at Reece and Jessie glaring at one another, then at Megan's flushed cheeks and dazed green eyes. Of course, that might depend on the players.

"Mom and Tyler win," Kara exclaimed. "Jessie took her hand off the circle first."

"Thank heaven," Megan breathed, resting her

forehead on his shoulder. "I thought that would never end."

"Spoilsport," he murmured back. "And we were having so much fun."

Her knee moved, nudging him in a strategic location. "Keep pushing and you'll be sorry," she said sweetly.

"You wouldn't."

"Wanna bet?"

"No." Tyler wouldn't bet anything when it came to Megan. How did a man court a woman who didn't recognize her own beauty? How did he make her believe in love and fairy tales and happy endings?

"Okay, now me and Jack against Mom and Tyler," Kara cried, handing the spinner to Eleanor. She grabbed Jack Carter's hand and dragged him to the mat.

Tyler decided that life just got better and better. "That's fine, Kara. Isn't that right, Megan?"

Megan smiled weakly. "Right. Fine."

To her eternal gratitude, the second game ended quickly when her foot slipped as she was trying to inch it around Jack's ankle. She went down, sweeping his leg out from under him. He fell forward, almost on top of her and Kara, but at the last minute Tyler yanked them both out of the way.

"Thanks," Megan mumbled.

"My pleasure." Tyler tugged on a lock of her hair, then turned to Kara. "You okay, kiddo?"

Kara looked at him so adoringly that Megan sighed. "I'm okay."

"That's good. You almost got squashed."

"I take exception to that comment," Jack said, getting up and dusting himself off. "She would have been bruised, not squashed. I ate a lot of lasagna at dinner, but not *that* much.''

"That's right, don't insult my husband," Toni called from her comfortable chair. She looked quite indignant. "I'm the only one in this room who's allowed to insult Jack."

"Uh…" Tyler's forehead creased in seeming puzzlement.

"It's a joke," Megan whispered.

His face cleared. "I didn't mean to step on your wifely toes, Toni."

Toni's eyes widened. "You mean I still have toes? I haven't seen them in weeks." She put a hand on her tummy and stuck her legs out in front of her. "By golly, you're right. That'll teach me not to eat so much."

"You aren't that big," Megan said. "I was bigger with Kara, and it all stuck out in front like I was giving birth to a beach ball."

"Aw, *Mom,*" Kara protested.

Tyler grinned. A few days ago it would have disturbed him to think about Megan carrying another man's child, but Kara was a great kid—smart, funny and too much like her mother for him not to appreciate her.

"That's done it. You know women, they're going to talk baby talk the rest of the night," Jack said, but he looked at his wife with unabashed love.

"Don't listen to him," Toni ordered, looking back with equal affection. "Jack has read every baby book on the market and practically drives our obstetrician crazy each time I'm pregnant. I think Jack could deliver a baby if he had to."

"But don't make me have to," her husband retorted.

Grinning, Tyler glanced at Megan. She'd clasped her arms around her waist, the way she did when she was upset, and her attention was fixed on the floor. "Megan?" he said quietly. He stroked the side of her face and she jumped.

"What?" Her green eyes had darkened to a deep, unhappy jade.

"You're a thousand miles away."

"I just…" She stopped and shook her head. "I'm going to see if anyone wants more dessert. Or coffee."

She slipped away so quickly he didn't have time to say anything.

Tyler cursed silently. There were so many layers of unhealed pain inside Megan. In some things she was wise and strong, in others so vulnerable that he ached.

He gave her a minute, then followed, fighting an illogical sense of hurt. Intellectually, he knew Megan was just trying to protect herself by keeping him at arm's length, but knowing and feeling something were two different things.

In the living room he glanced around and was starting to leave when one of his "cousins" pointed toward the door. "If you're looking for Megan, she's outside. Said she needed some fresh air."

Tyler nodded and walked to the French doors that opened into the garden.

It was sure handy having a matchmaking family.

The night air was chilly but Megan didn't mind after the warmth of the house. Though…it wasn't the house that had her overheated, it was Tyler. And old regrets she couldn't fix.

Across the garden she saw Tyler open the French doors and step outside. It didn't surprise her. Avoiding Tyler was like trying to avoid breathing—you could last a minute or two, but that was all. It was the same with ignoring him. He was too tall, too electric, too *male* for a woman to ignore, and she was furious because he was making it impossible to pretend she didn't feel anything for him.

She felt too much, that was the problem.

"What do you want?" she asked.

He sat on the bench and leaned back. "Just some fresh air."

"Of course," Megan muttered.

"Okay. I could tell you were upset when Toni and Jack talked about the baby," he murmured. "I was worried about you."

Megan stared into the distance. In the back of the house was an old orchard of fruit trees with rows of peaches and plums and apricots, and beyond were rolling oak-studded hills that gradually became steeper and steeper, until they were no longer hills, but mountains.

"It's nothing new...and nothing to worry about," she said finally. "Seeing Toni and Jack together is beautiful. I know it shouldn't make me feel sad, but it does."

"Because it reminds you that Brad didn't really want children," Tyler said perceptively. "And since he didn't want kids, I don't suppose he was supportive when you were pregnant with Kara. Was he?"

Megan shivered, but not from the cold. Brad had hated her being pregnant. The nasty things he'd said about her expanding waistline had devastated her. She'd desperately tried to rationalize his behavior, thinking that maybe he was jealous. Maybe he was afraid for her health. A thousand maybes, and none of them true.

"New life is a miracle," she whispered. "But all Brad saw was his wife getting fat and clumsier than ever."

"Not fat, *pregnant*. And never clumsy," Tyler said, an edge of anger in his voice. He lifted her across his lap, tucking her head into his shoulder. "I wish I could have seen you with Kara on the way. You would have been breathtaking."

"I've never been breathtaking."

"That's a matter of opinion, Megan." His fingers moved across her hair in soothing strokes. "You've always taken my breath away."

Megan closed her eyes, her senses filled with Tyler's warmth and masculine scent. She could allow the fantasy for a moment. Reality would intrude soon enough.

Megan measured coffee grounds into the fifty-cup percolator, getting it ready to start for breakfast in the morning.

It hadn't been easy, but she'd managed to stay away from Tyler for the past several hours. At least the reunion was going well and everyone was having a good time, especially her daughter. Kara's hard time would come later when she realized Tyler wasn't going to become a permanent fixture in their lives.

"Don't think about it," she told herself sternly.

The family had retired for the night, and the house

was silent except for the noises that all old houses made. She'd taken a protesting Kara to bed, sitting with her for the better part of an hour before going back downstairs to get things set up for the next morning.

The sound of someone coming down the back staircase made Megan sigh. She was as certain it was Tyler as she was certain the sun would come up in the morning.

"Yes?" she said when he appeared.

He looked around the kitchen, which she'd tidied after an evening of snacking and coffee-drinking. "I thought I'd find you down here."

"I might have gone to bed."

His head shook. "You're one of those people that plan ahead, getting stuff ready for the next day. Besides, I knocked at your bedroom and didn't get an answer."

Megan pressed her lips together. She probably wouldn't have answered Tyler if she *had* been in her bedroom. The time they'd spent alone in the garden had scared her, even more than kissing him had. She'd let her guard down too many times since he'd arrived, revealing things she'd never told anyone.

It was too confusing, dealing with him, her head and heart and body all clamoring for something different.

"I had fun tonight," he said.

"I'm glad."

Megan put the can of coffee into the refrigerator, then dusted her fingers. "I'm going to make sure the lights are off, then go upstairs."

"Good, I'll help," he said, following her out of the kitchen.

She rolled her eyes. "I don't need help with a couple of light switches."

"Then we can talk on the way."

There was a determination on his face that made Megan wince. She knew Tyler had questions, lots of them. Questions about her, about the past...about more things she didn't want to talk about. He could have pressed her in the garden, but instead he'd comforted her. Now he wanted answers.

"I'm tired, Tyler. Can't it wait?"

"No, because you'll come up with some other reason to avoid me. You're good at running away, but what I can't figure out is whether you're running from me or something else."

The accusation hit too close to home for Megan and she swallowed. "Please, don't."

"What is it, honey? Do you see Brad's ghost standing behind me? Is that it? He's been dead for two years. You have every right to rejoin the living."

If only it was that, Megan thought. But it wasn't Brad's ghost haunting her, it was her own inadequacy.

"Are you sure you don't miss Brad?" Tyler asked softly.

"*No.*" Megan said vehemently, then took a deep, calming breath. "It...it's been over two years. Kara and I had to move on."

It was a terrible answer, because if she'd still loved Brad she would have mourned his loss for the rest of her life. But slowly, over each day of their marriage, the love she'd felt for her husband had died. There were too many unkind words, too much arguing, and in the end, too many other women for it to survive.

"If you aren't still grieving over Brad, then why the hell are you running away from me?"

"I'm not—"

"Yeah, right. You're not running. Could have fooled me."

A wordless shriek escaped her throat. "What is it? What do you want?"

"I want to know why a beautiful woman, who's obviously devoted to her daughter and family, thinks she's lousy at marriage? It doesn't make sense."

"It's none of your business."

"Well, guess what? I'm making it my business."

"I am *not* discussing this with you."

"You can discuss it with me, or I can start asking questions in the family." Tyler instantly regretted his threat when the fury in Megan's eyes gave way to panic. "Please, just talk to me," he said more gently. "I already know Brad was a loser as a husband...what else did he do?"

She crossed her arms, shaking with emotion. "Fine. You want to know what happened? It's very simple. *Me*. That's all. I couldn't make it work."

"I don't believe that."

Megan impatiently dashed a tear from her cheek. "It's true. If he'd lived much longer, we would have gotten divorced. When Brad was killed, I hadn't seen him in over three days. You see, he was shacked up with his latest girlfriend—a girlfriend who had all the desirable qualities I lacked."

A hot, deep anger slashed through Tyler. Instead of dealing with his own deficiencies, Brad had done his best to destroy Megan, to tear her down to make himself feel better. Tyler had never liked his cousin, but he'd never thought the other man was capable of so much cruelty.

"I couldn't satisfy him," Megan whispered. "He said I was boring, with all the sex appeal of a—"

"Stop it." Tyler grabbed her shoulders. "You're a beautiful, desirable woman. And Brad was self-indulgent jackass. You were too good for him."

"I didn't—"

"No. You will not blame yourself. It's not your fault you married one of the few men on the planet too selfish and insecure to appreciate what a wonderful wife he had."

Torn, Megan stared into Tyler's eyes.

She wanted to believe there was nothing wrong with her, that she had as much to offer Tyler as any other woman. It was a sweet seduction she could barely resist.

"Honey…" he murmured, the nickname sounding like a caress. "Didn't it ever occur to you that Brad was the one who wasn't enough? That *he* failed *you?*"

"I never…quite thought of it that way," she said.

He grinned crookedly. "At least that's a start."

Chapter Nine

Tyler leaned against the wall and listened for movement in Megan's bedroom. It was even earlier than he'd gotten up the previous morning, but he didn't want to give her a chance to slip out without him.

If she planned to run.

A door further down the hallway opened up and Great-Grandmother Rose stepped out, leaning on her cane. She looked at him waiting opposite Megan's door and smiled knowingly.

"These things happen at their own pace. You mustn't be impatient," she said.

"That depends on how long you've been waiting."

Rose's faded blue eyes widened ever so slightly, then she nodded. "Yes. That would make a difference."

"What are you doing up so early?" Tyler asked.

"I'm going to write some letters. I'm old. I don't need as much sleep as you children."

Children?

Tyler grinned as Rose walked down the hall to a small second-floor parlor that Megan had furnished in a traditional Victorian style. Her B&B guests probably loved it—stepping into the parlor was like stepping back in time a hundred years.

Of course, the whole house had a welcoming feel. By contrast it made his bachelor status pretty damned boring. Sighing, Tyler put his head back against the wood paneling and closed his eyes. The clock on a nearby table ticked in cadence with his thoughts, measuring out the minutes the way the old clock in his bedroom had measured out the hours of the night.

Tick, tock. Tick, tock.

At first he'd blamed the unaccustomed ticking sound for his failure to sleep, but it was just a way of postponing the inevitable…deciding what to do about Megan.

He wanted Megan with an intensity that made his earlier passion for her seem like child's play. But she wasn't a piece of property or one of his business deals. She was a woman who'd been hurt. Badly. What made him think he could offer her anything she didn't already have?

"And what makes you think you could walk away again?" Tyler murmured, barely audibly in the early dawn stillness.

He couldn't, that's what.

He couldn't walk away from Megan again; the first time had been bad enough. This time Megan would have to decide whether he stayed or left.

Behind her door Tyler heard the faint sound of a voice, followed by a distinctive "marrrow." Obviously Beelzebub, the luckiest male in the house, having gotten to sleep with Megan.

Tyler waited, and after a few minutes the door opened.

"Hey," he said.

Megan jumped, but she didn't seemed surprised. "Planning on running?" she murmured.

"I will if you will. And I'm all set." He pointed to the reflective tape already fastened to his sweatshirt since she'd been so insistent about him wearing the stuff. "I've got to work off that food you keep feeding us."

"We like—"

"I know, the O'Bannons like to eat." He grinned, loving the early-morning drowsiness lingering in her eyes. "Did I say I was complaining?"

"No." Megan ran her palms over her thighs. "I'm glad you're enjoying the reunion."

"Very much, thanks to you."

"Oh." The compliment flustered her and she ducked her head. "That's…nice."

As he had the previous morning, Tyler let Megan set the pace of their run. A hard frost had glazed the landscape with a white mantle, making it hard to believe that in just a few hours it would be warm enough to play softball in a T-shirt and think of eating homemade ice cream with such pleasure.

Homemade ice cream.

For an instant Tyler's pace lagged behind Megan's as he remembered the flavor of strawberries and cream, lovingly prepared. He'd felt like a kid again, only happier than he'd ever been as a kid.

Megan looked back over her shoulder. "Is something wrong?"

"Not a thing. Hey, look out," he exclaimed as her foot went into an unseen pothole.

With an exclamation Megan sensed herself falling and threw out her hands. One hand and a knee hit the pavement before Tyler yanked her upright, somehow keeping them both from tumbling out of control. She gulped, stunned more by the contact with his hard body than the stinging pain in her hand.

A string of curses rang out over Megan's head. "Are you all right?" Tyler demanded finally, having run through all the curses Megan knew, and a few that she'd never heard before.

"Of course." Her voice was muffled against his sweatshirt.

Tyler's fingers threaded through her hair, pulling her face away from his chest. "You said that at the game, too, but you were hurt then."

"Uh…there isn't much difference between all right and barely hurt." She flexed her hand, trying not to wince at its soreness.

"Oh, *hell*," he said explosively as he pushed her away from him and looked down her legs.

Megan looked as well, but couldn't see anything worth getting so upset about. Bits of gravel clung to her knee and there was a small trickle of blood where a sharp edge had cut the skin, but it wasn't much. She'd gotten worse while running in charity events and had continued to the finishing line. If Tyler hadn't caught her she would have been much worse off, but he *had* caught her, so what was the big deal?

"Hey, I'm clumsy," she said, trying to sound flip, but the words cracked in her throat.

Tyler looked at her sharply. "You aren't clumsy," he said through gritted teeth. "And I don't want to hear one more blasted word that came out of Brad's stupid insensitive mind instead of yours.''

"I—"

"I mean it, Megan. My cousin dumped a load of crap on you because he knew he didn't deserve you. And I won't stand around and listen while you tear yourself down.''

She blinked. While she'd tried to diffuse the tension by saying she was clumsy, it really *had* come from Brad. She'd just heard it so often it was hard to forget.

"Come here," Tyler muttered, sweeping her into his arms before she could move an inch.

"Put me down. I'm perfectly all right. You aren't carrying me home.''

"Oh, be quiet," he growled. "I'm not carrying you home, I'm carrying you over there.''

Megan peered over his shoulder and saw one of the roadside monuments that punctuated the highways in the Gold Country. In this case, a natural spring had been diverted so that the water fell into a basin made of fitted rock, then down a culvert. She often stopped there during the summer when she was running, for a drink and to splash water on her face.

Tyler set her on the flat top of the rock wall and knelt to examine her knee more closely. He took a spotless white handkerchief from the pocket of his sweats and dipped it into the spring water, cleaning the tiny injury until he was satisfied it wasn't serious...which Megan could have told him without looking.

"Now, let me see your hand," he muttered.

Sighing because it wouldn't do any good to object, she stuck out her arm and saw his eyes narrow. The top surface of the skin was scraped, but not enough to draw blood. Under that, the base of her palm was turning blue, having taken the brunt of her minor tumble.

"I swear, you've cut ten years off my life in the last two days," Tyler said, gently probing the damage. "Flex your fingers."

"Nothing is broken," she declared, wiggling her fingers and twisting her wrist. "It's a little sore, that's all."

"I'll have Gene check it out when he gets here."

"Gene?"

"My friend the doctor."

"Oh...right. The one coming to see Eleanor. But I don't need a doctor," Megan said firmly.

"We'll let Gene decide that."

"I'm perfectly capable of making decisions on my own," she said, unable to keep an edge from her tone. "I'm not incompetent."

"I never said you were," Tyler said, sounding shocked. "But isn't it all right for me to worry about you?"

"Well—"

"Eleanor is going to be upset about the doctor, too. Do you think I'm treating her as if she's incompetent?"

Megan scowled. They both wanted Eleanor to see a doctor, and nobody in their right mind would consider her incompetent—stubborn and neglectful of her own well-being, perhaps, but never incompetent.

Tyler's thumb stroked across her palm, sending confused sensations up Megan's arm. It seemed almost sensual and she shifted uneasily.

"Did you know I read fortunes?" He lifted her

hand and kissed the center of it. "This is your love line," he whispered, drawing the tip of his tongue across her palm.

Megan's breath splintered as she reacted, both to the caress and to his warm proximity, her breasts tightening, her body growing warm and pliant.

She was right, the man was a menace. Women must do stupid stuff around Tyler, like mail him their underwear or drop by his apartment wearing a long coat...with nothing else beneath. They probably hoped he'd take one look and decide that maybe, just *maybe*, they were the women of his dreams.

Reluctantly, Megan pulled her hand free and stuck it behind her back. No point in tempting herself. "We'd better get on with our run."

"You shouldn't run with that knee hurt," Tyler said, his eyes changing from heavy-lidded sensuality to concern. "I'll run back and get my car."

"No you won't."

"Then we'll walk," he said stubbornly.

"Fine." Grumbling beneath her breath, Megan got up and started off in the direction of home. "See? I'm not even limping," she said.

Tyler caught up in two long strides. "There's no point in taking chances."

Some chances were more risky than others, Megan decided as she glanced at him...such as walking on an injured knee, and the chance of losing her heart to a man like Tyler.

It wasn't as if she was the best judge of men. Look at the mistake she'd made with Brad. Their marriage hadn't started off badly. They'd had the usual fights adjusting to one another, but nothing out of the ordinary.

The other stuff occurred slowly, with the last few months becoming pure hell. Not that she'd been all that happy before things got so awful, but she'd accepted the ups and downs—the ups being Kara and the O'Bannon family, the downs being Brad's endless criticism.

Her footsteps faltered until she was standing still. Wonderful. The "downside" of her marriage had been her own husband. What a lovely thought.

"Megan?"

"I wanted my marriage to work," she whispered. "I really did."

"I know, honey. It wasn't your fault Brad was such a skunk. Did you know I never liked him?" Tyler murmured, tucking her arm securely under his elbow. "I thought he was a jerk from the first day we met."

"I guess your judgment was better than mine."

"You were young and in love. We all do dumb things when we're young and in love."

"You did? That's hard to imagine."

"You bet." Tyler tugged at her arm until she began walking again. "I even have a tattoo to prove it." For a moment he looked chagrined by the confession, then he shrugged.

Megan laughed. "You have a tattoo? I don't believe it."

With a mock sigh, Tyler stopped again and peeled off his sweatshirt. He wasn't wearing a T-shirt beneath it and the breath caught in her throat, laughter forgotten. Every bit of him was tanned skin moving fluidly over hard muscles. A statue of a Greek god couldn't have been more compelling.

"See?" He pointed to his upper left arm where an

eagle in flight was tattooed on his biceps. Without thinking, Megan put out her fingers, lightly tracing the lines of the bird.

"How did love figure into this small piece of art?" she asked.

Tyler watched Megan's face, trying to tell if she was repelled by the tattoo, despite the way she touched him. "It was a stupid thing to do," he muttered. "I was eighteen, just out of boot camp, and trying to impress a girl with how macho and tough I could be. It was a huge mistake. I could have ended up with a deadly disease or bad infection—lots of guys do."

"At least you didn't get her name tattooed on your chest."

"Naw, I wasn't *that* much in love."

"Oh." Megan chuckled and dropped her hand. "I hate to think what you would have done if you'd been head over heels crazy about her."

Tyler didn't know, because the only time he'd been head over heels crazy about a woman was with Megan. He'd loved her for each of the nine years they'd been apart and was falling deeper by the minute.

"Maybe it evens out," he said lightly. "I got a tattoo, risking life and limb to do it, and you married a bozo who didn't deserve you."

"You mean love is hell?" she asked, moving forward again.

He pulled his sweatshirt back over his head and caught up again. "Love with the wrong person," he corrected. "With the right person you'll be surprised how good it could be."

How good it'll be with me, he wanted to add, but

they were in sight of the house and he needed any discussion of their future to be somewhere totally private.

Besides, it might be too soon.

All he could do was show her how beautiful and special she was, and pray that would be enough.

Everyone was sitting around after breakfast, groaning about eating too much and looking forward to lunch, when the doorbell rang.

Grady raised a sleepy eyelid. "I'll get that."

Megan exchanged glances with Tyler. They'd both gotten edgy as the morning passed, knowing the doctor would arrive at any time. "You stay. I'll take care of it," she said, getting up.

Tyler followed her to the door and greeted his friend with a strong handshake. "Gene Martinson, this is Megan O'Bannon."

She smiled and nodded at the other man, knowing instantly that Eleanor would like him...if they could get her to listen to him. Dr. Martinson looked like a homely, fifty-year-old version of Marcus Welby, with bushy white eyebrows and the same reassuring smile.

"It was nice of you to come down on short notice," she said.

"Nonsense. I love this part of the state—don't get here nearly enough. So, where is my patient?"

"What patient?"

Tyler whistled and turned his head. Eleanor had followed them to the foyer and she was looking none too pleased. "Now, Grams," he soothed. "Don't get upset, but I asked a friend to stop and take a quick look at you."

"Don't 'Grams' me, young man," she scolded. At the same time she looked inordinately pleased that Tyler had finally called her something other than "Eleanor" or "ma'am."

"Please let the doctor examine you," Megan pleaded softly. "Everyone is so worried. You didn't eat anything at lunch again today."

Eleanor let out a long-suffering sigh. "All right. But you can't drag this poor man down here without putting him up for the night. The doctor and I will chat while you two geniuses figure out where he's going to sleep. The house is a bit crowded, you know."

"Gene can have my room," Tyler offered.

Gene can have my room?

Where did Tyler think he was going to sleep? Megan rapped her fingers on her legs as Eleanor and Dr. Martinson went into the front parlor and chased everyone out except Grady, who flashed a delighted victory symbol at Tyler with his fingers.

"Isn't that nice?" Tyler asked. "Eleanor upgraded us to geniuses."

"Whatever," Megan muttered. She climbed the stairs, thinking furiously.

"I thought you'd be happy that she agreed to talk to a doctor," Tyler said.

"I'm very happy."

"You don't look happy. What's wrong now?"

"Nothing."

Tyler's sigh sounded just as long-suffering as Eleanor's had been. "Honey, you've got something bothering you, and I want to know what it is."

She turned around and glared as he followed her into her bedroom. "Okay, if Dr. Martinson is sleeping in your room, I want to know where you think *you're* going to sleep?"

"Oh." Tyler thought for a moment. He could tell what Megan was thinking and his answer had to be just right or he'd make things worse. Much as he'd love taking her to bed for the next couple of centuries, he wasn't going to do it until there was a gold ring on her finger.

His gold ring.

On the other hand, she needed to understand how much he wanted her. Hell, want was an understatement. He was going crazy thinking about how soft and warm she felt in his arms and how much he needed her back in them again.

"I wasn't thinking that far ahead," Tyler said. "But don't you have a spare couch around, or at least an unused sleeping bag?"

Megan wet her lips with the tip of her tongue, looking uncertain. "You can't sleep on a couch."

"Of course I can. Believe me, I've slept on worse."

"Then you didn't think..." She glanced at her own bed and turned pink.

Tyler had been doing his best not to look at Megan's bed, since just looking was enough to get him aroused. Actually, it was the thought of Megan *in* the bed that had him burning, but seeing it wouldn't help matters.

He cupped her face in his hands, his thumb stroking across her lips. "Honey, there isn't anything I'd rather do than make love with you, but a decent man waits for an invitation. I'd never presume something so arrogant. Besides, with the family around, it would be awkward."

"Uhm...yes."

"Of course, someday I'd love having you all to myself." Tyler kissed her forehead, then her nose, and finally the sweet curve of Megan's lips. He pulled her closer and trailed another series of kisses along her jaw, whispering sensual fantasies into her ear.

Despite the embarrassed warmth creeping across her skin, Megan put her arms around Tyler's neck and swayed against him. She'd been married for six years, but she'd never heard such sweet, sexy propositions.

And outrageous.

Some of Tyler's ideas sounded impossible...but it would be fun finding out.

If she had the nerve.

Megan stiffened slightly. Once she'd been confident and willing to take chances, but everything was different now. Except with Tyler. At the moment he made her feel as if anything could happen.

It turned out that Gene Martinson, or "Dr. Gene" as he insisted they call him, was a big hit with the O'Bannon family. He had a quick wit and the gift of really focusing his attention on a person. What they particularly appreciated was the news that Eleanor was likely suffering from gallstones and not something more serious.

Of course, gallstones were serious enough if complications set in, but he said they'd check her out in San Francisco later the next week and schedule the surgery immediately.

"Everything seems to be going well," Tyler said, sitting next to Megan at one of the picnic tables.

"Grady is happy and I think Eleanor has even for-given us."

"You," she said. "She'd forgive you anything."

He lifted her hand, kissed the bruised skin at the base of her palm, and laced their fingers together. "Have you noticed how taken Gene is with Cousin Ruby? They're really hitting it off. Wouldn't it be something if they got together?"

Ruby Varner was a distant cousin on Eleanor's side of the family. She was a handsome woman in her late forties. She'd spent the better part of the last twenty-five years in the Peace Corps, which it turned out was a particular interest of Gene Martinson's.

"He's only been here for an hour," Megan said dryly. "I think we should wait before sending the wedding invitations."

"How about love at first sight?"

With her free hand Megan flicked at the red-checked tablecloth. Did she believe in love at first sight? Something had certainly happened to her the first time she'd seen Tyler—unfortunately she'd been engaged to another man at the time.

What would have happened if she'd met him first?

She stared down at their joined hands and tried to believe he truly desired her. Could they have a future together? Something real and different from her first marriage?

Her judgment about men might be faulty, but it was obvious he was opposite from Brad in the im-portant things. Maybe Tyler wasn't that comfortable with family, but he was trying. And he was basic and down to earth and willing to work hard for what he wanted.

"Have you seen the way Ruby is looking at Dr.

Gene?" Toni asked as she walked by. "I tell you, it's fate. They're perfect for each other."

"I agree," Tyler said. He chuckled and nudged Megan with his elbow.

Megan let out an exasperated sigh. The O'Bannons were die-hard romantics, every single one of them. Even Tyler. How could a person think rationally around them? She wanted to be practical and sensible and they were confusing her with their passion for happily-ever-after.

Which was fine, except *they* wouldn't have the broken hearts if things didn't work out with Tyler.

"It would be nice if we could get away later," he murmured after Toni was out of earshot. "So we can talk."

She took three quick breaths and shook her head. "We're playing softball later, remember?"

"Maybe after the game."

"I don't think so...we'll be working on dinner." Megan untangled their fingers and got up. "I better get things moving for the barbecue. We're having ribs today and it's a big job."

"I'll help," Tyler said.

Naturally.

But it was hard to stay annoyed when he smiled and tucked a strand of her hair behind her ear—the same ear he'd whispered such sinfully wonderful suggestions into just two hours before.

He made her feel beautiful and graceful and desired...all the things a woman wanted to feel. She tried to remember if another man had ever once made her feel so alive, but if one had, it was nothing compared to Tyler.

Which made the risk that much greater.

Chapter Ten

"When do you want to leave for the park?" Megan asked three hours later.

"Not me," Jack said. He stretched out his legs and winked at his wife. "I'm feeling lazy. Think I'll skip the game."

Megan frowned. It was strange, but everyone was saying the same thing—no softball for them, they wanted to loaf after eating such a rich meal. This family never gave up their softball matches; along with Kara, they were passionate about games of any kind.

Eyes narrowed, she looked at Tyler chatting with a group of the family she hadn't spoken with yet. His standoffish days seemed to be over, because they were smiling, nodding and making approving gestures.

"Those ribs were delicious," Dr. Gene said. "Not what I would recommend as a healthy heart diet, but first rate. Was that your own barbecue sauce, Megan?''

''Uhm, yes.''

''Do you have any special ingredients?''

Distracted, Megan turned around. ''Yes. Lots of onions, brown sugar and bourbon whiskey.''

''Bourbon, eh?'' Dr. Gene chuckled. ''Tyler said I'd like you.''

Tyler said...

Megan focused more intently on the doctor. He did have a goofy expression on his face when he looked at Ruby—kind of a thunderstruck ''where have you been all my life?'' dazzle in his eyes. And Ruby seemed equally taken with him.

''When did Tyler mention me?'' Megan asked.

''When he called yesterday. He couldn't stop talking about you.'' Dr. Gene shook his head. ''I've known Tyler for six years and I've never heard him speak about a woman like that.''

''O-oh?''

''Oh, yes. I couldn't wait to meet you.''

Heat grew in Megan's face, and with a mumbled excuse she fled toward the house. Things were out of control. *She* was out of control, acting like a girl with her first crush on a boy. *Does he like me? What did he say?* Lord, she'd never been this bad, even when she *was* a girl.

In the kitchen she found various female members of the family trying to decide what to do with the leftovers.

''Should we put it in the freezer?'' Toni asked, staring at a mound of baby back ribs, dripping with bourbon barbecue sauce. ''There must be thirty pounds left.''

"And twenty pounds of chicken from yesterday," Eleanor said. "Not to mention all that lasagna."

Megan looked at the barbecued meat with an equal amount of disinterest. She was so stirred up about Tyler that her stomach wouldn't tolerate food, much less something like ribs.

"We won't cook tonight, we'll eat leftovers," Eleanor announced.

"But—"

"Leftovers," Eleanor said firmly. "And you're not to step foot in this kitchen the rest of the day. I think you should take Tyler out to the O'Bannon gold mine this afternoon. He never saw it when he lived with us."

Megan instantly shook her head. That place was special. It represented the hopes and dreams and values of the family. In three generations she was the only O'Bannon bride who hadn't been married in the valley—Brad preferring a society wedding—and seeing it with Tyler would only be a reminder of something that would never come true.

Through the window Megan saw Tyler walking toward the house. He had a pleased look on his face...sort of like a cat who'd gotten the cream. Excitement and a significant amount of fear danced on her unsettled tummy; the fear she understood, the excitement was harder to comprehend.

"What about softball?" she asked.

"From what I hear, the game has been cancelled," Toni said. Megan's eyes narrowed, but the other woman was stretching plastic wrap over a bowl of ambrosia salad and didn't look up.

The door opened and Tyler stepped inside. "Great weather we're having. Much too nice to waste."

Eleanor nodded. "That's right. I was just suggesting that Megan take you out to see the old gold mine. You've never been there, have you?"

"No, but it sounds like fun." Tyler looked at Megan, his smile stopping just short of smug.

Her heart fluttered in her throat. She was being manipulated by a bunch of kindhearted con artists.

She pressed a hand to her midriff. "Maybe everyone would like to go."

"You're the ambitious ones," Toni said, getting up and rubbing the small of her back. "You even went running this morning, while the rest of us were fast asleep in our beds."

"We should ask Kara—"

"She's talked Ruby and Gene into playing horseshoes," Tyler said. "You'll never drag her away. Let's go." He put a hand on her back and urged her toward the front of the house.

"Tyler—"

"Megan," he returned in the same tone, only louder. "No more excuses. I want to see this gold mine."

Sighing in defeat, Megan went to the foyer closet and pulled out her purse. "We should drive up in my Chevy Blazer. There isn't a good road into the valley."

They walked down to the blue four-wheel-drive Blazer and she automatically held out the keys.

"You should drive," Tyler said. "Unless your hand is too sore," he added.

Megan looked down at the keys dangling from her fingers and sensed her world tilting. Brad had always insisted on being behind the wheel, whether they were driving across town, or across the state.

Tyler put his finger on Megan's chin and lifted her face. Her eyes were confused and it worried him before he recognized the source. "I get it, Brad was a jerk about cars, too."

"He didn't trust me. He said—"

"It doesn't matter what he said," Tyler interrupted gently. "I'm not Brad." It was a simple statement, yet it was the one thing Megan needed to understand more than anything else.

He wasn't Brad.

He had both his faults and good qualities. He had money to burn, but at heart he was a rough ex-soldier with callouses on his hands and a tattoo on his arm. And he'd accepted that none of that mattered, because he also wasn't the kind of man who would deliberately hurt a woman.

What mattered was Megan, and whether she wanted *him.*

"Don't guys prefer driving?" she asked, but her hand dropped to her side, still holding the keys.

"Sometimes," Tyler admitted. "Only for me it's because I think I should be strong and protective and do the work rather than sitting idly by. Hey, I never claimed to be politically correct."

He was pleased to see a tiny smile tugging at Megan's lips. "Nobody is totally politically correct."

"Especially since *politically correct* changes every five minutes," Tyler agreed. "You just do your best. Naturally I do better than my best at work, not wanting any of my employees to think I'm a sexist."

"Naturally."

Megan was quiet for the first twenty minutes of the drive, then she glanced at him. "Tyler, do you think men and women are naturally at odds with each other?''

''No. I think we're two halves of a perfect whole.''
Two halves of a perfect whole.

Megan shivered at the thought of being part of a perfect whole with Tyler. It could never happen, yet he'd shown her one thing...intimacy with a man didn't have to be a total disaster. With the right man. A man like Tyler, who didn't think only of himself.

''Where is this gold mine?'' he asked after another minute. ''I remember it being mentioned when I lived here, but nothing else.''

''Oh.'' Megan laughed nervously. ''That's sort of a joke. How much do you know about the O'Bannon's history in California?''

''I'm afraid it didn't interest me as a teenager, and later there was never time.'' Tyler shifted in his seat, preferring to watch Megan, who was far more decorative than the scenery. Not that the scenery lacked anything...it just wasn't Megan.

''The first O'Bannons came west during the 1850s to dig for gold. When they got here they staked out a claim, then realized they'd make more money feeding the miners. At a dollar for a slice of bread, it probably didn't take much math.''

Tyler whistled. ''Nice ancestors I've got. Sounds like extortion.''

''No, they were good people. I've looked into the old records and they charged much less than their competitors. Peg and Rory made quite a bit, but no great fortune. And they never let anyone go hungry because they couldn't pay.''

''Why did you do so much research?''

Megan seemed surprised. ''They're Kara's ancestors, too. I thought she should know about her family."

They're Kara's ancestors, too.

Tyler smiled. If he convinced Megan to marry him, then his stepdaughter would share his family roots. It was a nice feeling, though it didn't make any real difference. Kara was Megan's daughter, and that was enough. "So what about the gold mine?"

"Well, they were so busy hauling provisions to the gold fields, they never had time to work the claim."

She slowed the Blazer, turning onto a narrow gravel lane. It seemed familiar and Tyler realized it was the old road that went along Grady and Eleanor's property line.

"Do the O'Bannons still own the land? The original stake?" he asked, surprised.

"Of course, they'd never sell it."

The Blazer crept across an old wood bridge over the creek, and then up the hill. A genuine curiosity was growing in Tyler. Eleanor had insisted the O'Bannon gold mine was the place he should propose to Megan, saying he'd understand once he got there.

"Anyway," Megan continued. "After a few years Peg was tired of raising a growing family out of a wagon, so she wanted to build a house and work the claim. Then she got up here, and decided the land was too beautiful to destroy by mining." She slowed the vehicle to a stop. "Take a look and you'll understand."

Tyler tore his gaze away from Megan and looked out the window. A small, secluded valley curved out in front of them, a silver stream murmuring through the middle. Along one side ran a swath of aspens that quivered gold in the sunlight. It was the most peaceful place he'd ever seen.

"You're right, it's something," he murmured. "Did they build their house here?"

"The first one—in the clearing down there. Later on they tore it down and built the house where Eleanor and Grady live."

She got out and walked down a path overgrown with grass seared golden brown by the summer heat and the coming of winter. The path ended at a clearing on the floor of the valley, close enough to the creek to hear the cheerful babble of the water. A granite boulder at the clearing's edge caught Tyler's attention and he crouched in front of a brass plate mounted on it.

"May each generation of our children's children find joy in this valley," the inscription read. "And may all their sorrows be offered into the Lord's keeping. Rory and Margaret O'Bannon."

Rory and Margaret.

These were *his* ancestors, his great-great-great-grandparents. The ancestors who linked him to Grandmother Rose and Grady and Eleanor and Toni, and all the rest.

"The old plaque eroded away," Megan said. "The one Rory and Peg put up. Grady and Eleanor mounted that one about thirty years ago. But it's identical to the first."

Tyler looked up. "And the family has always kept the valley just like it is? No mining or development, other than the first house?"

Megan nodded and smoothed the skirt of her dress. It was green and soft and feminine and the light shone through the thin fabric, illuminating the sweet lines of her body. She was so beautiful it took his breath away.

Tyler glanced again at the plaque, and it was as if everything settled into place at once. *This* was what Megan had been trying to tell him for the past several days.

He *belonged.*

These were his ancestors. The roots he'd always wanted and refused to see.

Tyler traced the words on the plaque, for the first time in his life feeling truly connected, not only to a family, but to a place. He was one of Rory and Margaret's "children's children," belonging to a generation distantly separated in time, but still the recipient of their hopes for the future.

And he had a strange conviction that Rory and Margaret were smiling at him from heaven that very minute, offering their encouragement and blessing.

Standing, Tyler put his hand in his pocket, touching the small jewelry box he'd brought from San Francisco. He'd purchased the ring years ago, an antique ruby and diamond band that was as unique as the woman he'd always wanted to wear it.

"We need to talk," he said softly.

He could see the muscles in Megan's throat as she swallowed. "I don't…that is, maybe we should go back."

"Back home? I think I'm already home."

Tyler smiled and caught her hand as she took a step backward. This might be his only chance for them to talk privately and he wasn't giving it up. Yet more than that, he now understood why Eleanor had wanted him to propose here. The bright threads of tradition were woven through the valley, traditions of love and permanence and devotion.

Returning to San Francisco wasn't an option, not without Megan and her daughter. But then, he didn't want to leave at all. He wanted to live with her in that great big house that Megan and the O'Bannons had restored with such love. It was far more appealing than the city.

Home was where you belonged, and he knew with utter certainty that he belonged with Megan and Kara and any other children that might come along.

"The valley is special," Megan said, discreetly trying to pull her hand from Tyler's. Finally she gave up trying to be discreet and yanked.

"Not just the valley," he drawled, ignoring her efforts. "You're special, too."

"No, I'm not," she muttered, the denial coming automatically as she pried at the strong fingers holding her wrist.

"I told you never to say things like that." The warning came in such a conversational tone that it didn't register on her consciousness until *Tyler* gave her a good yank and she ended up in his arms, her body pressed to him from her breasts to her knees.

"T-Tyler?"

He stared at her mouth until she licked her lips in nervous reaction, then he kissed her so hard she was arched backward over his forearm. It occurred to Megan as she returned the embrace with equal enthusiasm that she might have been hoping he would kiss her.

Minutes later they both came up for air and Megan blinked up at Tyler. She didn't have the slightest notion what was going on, but it was the nicest kiss she'd ever gotten.

"I suppose you want an apology?" he asked huskily.

"If you apologize I'm going to hit you," she muttered, meaning it with all her heart. He'd apologized after their kiss in the pantry, and she didn't want to hear it again.

"Point taken. Now, about what we were discussing…?"

"We weren't discussing anything."

"Okay, let's go back to what I *wanted* to discuss with you." He smiled and her pulse doubled its already racing speed. "I want to marry you."

Shock widened her eyes and she stared.

A proposal.

Okay, she'd been expecting something, but not a proposal, not really. Maybe a proposition, but not marriage. "You're crazy."

"Only about you."

Megan pushed against Tyler, this time managing to break free. "No."

"That's a hasty answer. Think about it until the answer is yes."

"It won't ever be yes," she hissed, her old insecurities rushing up, threatening to engulf her. She wanted to marry Tyler more than she'd wanted anything in her life, but it was too much risk. If he ever looked at her with disappointment in his face it would kill her.

"Megan, you—"

"No." She backed up, nearly stumbling into the shallow waters of the creek before Tyler caught her. "You haven't been listening to me. I don't want to

get married again. I messed up one marriage, I'm not messing up another.''

"For God's sake, Megan, you're the one who isn't listening. You didn't mess up anything. Brad was an immature egotist who didn't deserve to come near you. He's gone now, and I'm sorry about that for Kara and the rest of the family, but I won't let him come between us. I'm a stubborn man, Megan. You have no idea how stubborn.''

"I'm not marrying you. If you're worried about Eleanor, then don't. She has Reece and Jessie's wedding to look forward to, she doesn't need ours.''

"I thought we'd settled this,'' Tyler said, annoyed. "Proposing has nothing to do with Eleanor. I've wanted you since the first moment we met, and I'll be damned if I'll wait another nine years to marry you.''

"You couldn't have…'' Megan's protest trailed and she looked at him uncertainly.

"Yes, I could have and I did. I wanted you so bad I would have cheerfully pushed Brad off a cliff if there'd been one that was handy.''

"You never said anything. You just looked at me and disapproved. I know you thought I shouldn't marry him—and don't deny it.''

Tyler sighed. They'd gotten their messages wrong all those years before and they were still getting them wrong. "Megan, of course I didn't think you should marry him. I thought you should marry *me*.''

"Then why didn't you say so?'' she asked crossly.

"I couldn't. You were engaged to Brad.''

Megan gritted her teeth. "Is this some of that male honor nonsense?''

"It isn't nonsense.''

"It is if I married the wrong man!" Her retort rang out across the clearing and she winced. She might as well have announced she had feelings for him.

Tyler stroked Megan's face with his fingers, then rubbed the ball of his thumb across her lips. They were pink and swollen from his caresses, reminding him that he'd much rather kiss her again than dig up the past. But there were things that had to be said first.

"Megan, you're everything I've ever wanted, but we met at the wrong time, when I was too tangled up with my pride and honor and a chip on my shoulder because I thought I was the outsider. Please...will you tell me how you felt when we met?"

"Uh, well, you scared me."

His brows drew together in a puzzled frown. "I scared you? I know you said I seemed stern, but why would that scare you?"

Megan put her hand over Tyler's, keeping his palm cupped to her cheek. Hope was bubbling up inside her, despite her best efforts to stay sensible.

"You were so intense," she whispered. "So gorgeous and sexy, I was completely tongue-tied whenever you looked at me. I knew I was out of my depth around you, and then you seemed so disapproving."

His frown eased into a smile. "Did you think about kissing me?"

"Yes," Megan said reluctantly. "I always felt a little guilty about it, but it wasn't as if I did anything."

"There's nothing to feel guilty about," Tyler said. With his free hand he brushed the hair from her forehead. "If Brad had been a different kind of man he'd still be alive and you would have loved him forever. But he's gone and I'm here, and I'll do whatever it takes to show you how special you are.''

With all her heart she wanted to believe him. Brad had never once made her *feel* beautiful, even when they were courting. But with Tyler…it was different. She felt beautiful when he looked at her, in a way she'd never felt before.

Ultimately, wasn't that what it was all about? Knowing the man you love sees you as attractive and desirable? That no matter what the years bring, you'll always be exciting and wonderful to him?

"Ah, Megan, I love you so much."

It was the first time Tyler had said anything about love and Megan thought her heart would leap right out of her throat it was beating so madly. "You…do?"

Tyler drew her closer, his gaze never losing contact with hers. "Of course I love you. Please say there's a chance for us. You're everything I ever dreamed of having. Don't ask me to give you up now.''

In his eyes Megan saw a reflection of herself, both the girl she'd been, and the woman she'd become. And in them she was beautiful and precious, the answer to his dreams.

"Please trust me, honey."

Tears swam in Megan's eyes and she threw her arms around Tyler's neck. "I love you, too," she whispered over and over.

Relief swept through Tyler and he breathed a silent prayer of thanks. Clearing his throat, he tugged her arms free from his neck and stepped back.

"Tyler?" she said, clearly puzzled.

"I want to do this right, because it's the last proposal I'm ever making." He took the velvet jewelry box from his pocket and sank down on one knee. "I love you, Megan O'Bannon. I want to live with you in that splendid old Victorian and be a father to Kara. Will you make me the happiest man on the planet and marry me?"

"You're being a little old-fashioned, aren't you?"

"Traditional, my love. Traditional. There's nothing old-fashioned about being madly, passionately in love with the most wonderful woman ever born."

"Isn't that extravagant?"

Tyler would have been frustrated, but he loved seeing the spark of confidence in Megan that let her tease him. "It isn't the least bit extravagant."

"Oh. Okay. How much time do I have to make up my mind?"

"None," he growled. "I want to be able to carry you over the threshold on our wedding night, but I have a rock digging into my knee. Say yes before I'm permanently disabled."

"I..." Megan would have prolonged the teasing, but underlying the laughter in Tyler's face was a sensual heat that made her lightheaded. "Yes."

Within a second she was in his arms and he sank down into the soft grass at the creek bank, rolling till she was lying on his chest. Several long, sweet kisses later he sighed with satisfaction, nudging her more squarely on top of him.

"That's better," he said.

"Mmmm."

"Want to see your ring?" Tyler popped the box open and took it out. "I bought this for you before your wedding. It was right after I sold my first big piece of property. The minute I saw it, I had to get it. I know it wasn't logical since you were engaged but I've never been logical about you."

Nine years...the enormity of Tyler loving her all that time still stunned Megan. And the ruby engagement ring, made of antique red gold, was another shock. "It's beautiful," she gasped.

Tyler slipped the circlet over her third finger, nodding in satisfaction when it proved to be a perfect fit. "It's over a hundred years old," he murmured.

"It's perfect." Megan admired the ring, then propped her chin on her hands and looked into her fiancé's eyes. "When do you want to get married?" she asked.

"Soon." He smiled, a wickedly pleased smile. "I have it on good authority that engaged people don't always sleep together, so I don't want the wedding to be a second later than it has to be. I've taken enough cold showers for one lifetime."

She grinned back, remembering her lecture to Kara on the first day of the reunion. "All right. I don't think it takes long to get a marriage license in California. We could get married on Monday or Tuesday. Can you wait till then?"

"Just barely." They shared another, long, slow kiss. "Will we be able to get someone to marry us here in the valley?"

Megan nodded, so happy she could barely speak. "That won't be a problem. Jack Carter is a preacher. I'm sure he and Toni will stay another couple of days."

"A preacher?" Tyler dropped his head back and laughed. "I should have guessed. Now...let's go tell the family they were successful in matchmaking us together.''

''They'll be in heaven.''

''That's okay...I got there first.'' And Tyler held Megan against his heart where she'd stay for the rest of his life.

This was one happily-ever-after they'd make sure came true. *Together.*

Epilogue

"To the bride and groom. May their joy only grow." Reece O'Bannon lifted his champagne in the air, and his toast was echoed in the voices of the surrounding family.

Megan leaned against Tyler's chest, smiling through her tears. The O'Bannons had proved they could move mountains, putting together a dream wedding over the weekend.

But the O'Bannons knew just about everyone in a three-county area, so it wasn't that difficult calling in favors and getting everyone from a caterer to photographers on such short notice.

Along with Dr. Gene Martinson, the whole family had made arrangements to stay for the Monday-afternoon ceremony, though they'd discreetly assured Megan they'd be gone for the wedding night. Eleanor and Grady were keeping Kara for the evening, and they'd all head for San Francisco the next day.

Eleanor had balked, saying a one-night honeymoon was ridiculous, but Tyler assured her he'd take Megan on a fabulous trip as soon as possible. And anyway, how could they enjoy a honeymoon if they were worried about her?

Megan closed her eyes and tipped her face to the warm sunshine. This was one of those moments in life when things were practically perfect.

Light kisses fluttered across her closed eyes and she smiled dreamily.

"Happy, my dear wife?"

"What do you think?"

"I think you're so beautiful my breath catches each time I look at you."

She looked into Tyler's face, then reached up and kissed him back. "I'm so glad you came to the reunion," she whispered against his mouth and felt him smile.

"So am I."

The click of a camera shutter barely registered, along with all the other noises of wedding revelers and the natural sounds of the breeze and creek water flowing nearby. But after a moment Megan sighed and stepped back.

"I'm going to see how Eleanor is doing," she said.

Tyler watched as his bride slipped away, stopped frequently by enthused hugs and kisses of their mutual family. She wore a soft white dress that hung in graceful folds to mid-calf, and her hair was piled on top of her head in a soft, feminine style. She was luminous. If he had awakened in a fairy tale, he couldn't have been happier.

His gaze settled briefly on the granite boulder bearing the inscription from Margaret and Rory

O'Bannon. He'd learned that Peg's favorite flowers were pink roses, the same as Megan's, and he'd arranged to have the monument massed by a bank of pink rosebuds.

Thank you, he said silently, grateful beyond words for the loving legacy they'd passed down to their family,

Further away, sitting alone on a rock by the creek, was Kara. She'd got a streak of dirt on her fancy new green dress and she was tossing pebbles into the water, one by one.

Tyler took off his shoes and socks and sat next to her, sticking his feet into the cool current of water. "Hey, kiddo."

"Hey."

Since Kara had been so enthusiastic about him marrying her mother, he was worried to see her quiet and withdrawn now that the deed was done. Normally Kara was anything but quiet.

"What gives?" he asked, nudging her with his shoulder.

"You're gonna be nice to my mummy, aren't you?"

The question startled Tyler so much he couldn't say anything for a moment, then he nodded. "Of course, I am. I love your mother. I've loved her since before you were born. Why?"

"Because my daddy wasn't very nice to her."

Tyler's forehead creased. The previous night he'd talked a long while with Megan about her first marriage. Her own childhood had been marred by vicious battles between her parents, and she'd tried to protect her daughter from the uncertainty she'd always felt growing up. Apparently Kara had known things were bad, anyway.

"Uhm...what do you mean, Kara?"

"I don't remember very well, but he made Mummy cry a lot. She'd come out of her room and her eyes would be all red, but she'd pretend nothing was wrong." Kara stared at her toes, then wiggled them in the water. "She never says bad things about him, only sometimes I hear people talking and...and I don't think my daddy was a very nice man."

Tyler took a deep breath and searched for the right words. This was his first test as a stepfather and he didn't want to blow it. But before he could say anything, Kara shook her head and looked at him with a very adult expression on her face.

"It's okay, because my mummy is *wonderful*," she said fiercely. "Grandma Eleanor says I'm the luckiest girl ever to have a mummy like that."

"And I'm the luckiest man ever to be married to her, and to have you for my little girl. It's all right, isn't it? For me to be your new daddy?"

"Uh-huh." It wasn't an enthusiastic response, but it was better than nothing.

"You know...," Tyler said slowly. "Your mother and I are probably going to argue sometimes, but that's all right. I promise we'll always make up, and that I will never do anything to hurt her. I think your mother is wonderful, too. So, do we have a deal? We'll take care of her together."

Kara thought about it for a long minute, then she stuck out her hand and they shook.

Standing a few feet away, Megan fought to keep tears from spilling down her cheeks. She'd known something was bothering Kara, but she hadn't been able to get her daughter to open up. Tyler lifted his head and their gazes met. She gave him a watery smile.

"So, do you guys want homemade ice cream, or what?" she asked huskily.

"Yummers," Kara cried. She jumped up, gave both Tyler and her mother a big kiss, then darted toward the food.

Tyler came more slowly, but his kiss was longer and very adult, to the point her pulse pounded dizzily through her head. "It's getting late," he murmured.

"Y-yes?"

"I was thinking we might stay a bit longer, then head back to the house."

The heat in his eyes promised it would be a very long, very passionate evening and she shivered with a combination of anticipation and tension. "That sounds...fine."

"But I don't want you to miss anything here," he added, a faint concern creeping into his voice.

"I won't."

Now that they were getting closer to the actual wedding night, Megan found her nerves were misbehaving with a vengeance. It was like being a virgin again, because nothing with Tyler would be comparable to the past.

In no time they were saying goodbye to everyone, kissing Kara and promising to see her in the morning. At Megan's request, Tyler drove the Blazer back home. She was afraid of landing them in a ditch, the way her hands were shaking.

"It's going to be all right," Tyler said after he'd parked in front of the Victorian home. "Wait here for a minute."

He got out and went to the front door of the house, unlocking the door and leaving it open. He then lifted her in his arms and carried her inside, his powerful arms holding her securely.

"You do that very nicely," she murmured.

"I do other things nicely, too." To her surprise, Tyler didn't set her down, instead turning and nudging the door closed with his foot. He then kissed her, grinned, and took the staircase running.

Megan giggled and clung to his neck. "You're crazy," she declared as he charged down the hall to the master bedroom.

"It's one of my best qualities."

Tyler put her on the bed and she looked around, her eyes widening. Someone had been there since she'd left a few hours before; there were pink roses and ferns in every nook and cranny, scenting the air, turning the room into a garden bower.

"It's lovely," she whispered.

"I wanted a proper setting for you." Tyler leaned over her, kissing her, his hands roaming freely over her body until a few minutes later Megan gasped and crossed her arms over her breasts.

"How did you do that?" she demanded.

Tyler tossed her wedding dress over his shoulder. "Good hands." His tie and shirt followed the dress in short order.

Torn between laughter and embarrassment, Megan grabbed for a pillow to cover herself, then stopped. He would see the rest of her soon enough, so she lay back, trying not to stiffen or seem unwilling. Heck, she was very willing, she just wasn't sure what to do next.

"Don't be nervous," Tyler urged, yet he was a

little nervous himself. He wanted Megan so much he was afraid he'd lose control.

Two scraps of white covered her breasts and hips—a silk bra and a pair of lacy French-cut panties that strained his breathing to the point of strangulation. But it was the satin garters and silk hose that tempted him the most.

He removed the last of his own clothing, then eased the bra from her body. "I love garters," Tyler murmured. He unfastened the hose from Megan's left leg, stroking the soft skin of her inner thigh as he rolled the sheer silk down. "They're so sexy. Especially taking them off."

Megan looked down. Tyler's eyes were dark, almost fierce as he trailed his hands back to the fastenings on her right leg, teasing her with small forays into intimate territory. When his fingers hooked the elastic of her panties she lifted her hips and let him remove them as well.

He was…magnificent. She couldn't question the depth of his desire for her, it was too proud and blatant not to recognize.

Tyler rested his fists on the mattress, dragging breaths into his lungs. "I wasn't planning on using anything," he muttered finally. "So tell me if you don't want to get pregnant right away, or at all. It's your choice. We can fill this house with babies if that's what you want, or be content with our daughter."

Our daughter.

The confidence Megan had thought was gone forever swelled inside her and she smiled. "Kara was born in late September. If we work quickly, she could have a baby brother or sister by her birthday."

Tyler pressed his hand to her belly with a possessive, tender expression. ''Then we won't use anything.''

''Just love,'' Megan agreed, tugging him into her arms.

* * * * *

Don't miss the reprisal of
Silhouette Romance's popular miniseries

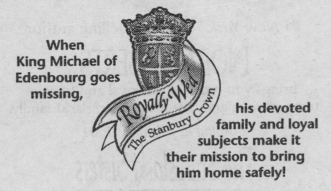

When King Michael of Edenbourg goes missing, his devoted family and loyal subjects make it their mission to bring him home safely!

Their search begins March 2001 and continues through June 2001.

On sale March 2001: **THE EXPECTANT PRINCESS** by bestselling author **Stella Bagwell** (SR #1504)

On sale April 2001: **THE BLACKSHEEP PRINCE'S BRIDE** by rising star **Martha Shields** (SR #1510)

On sale May 2001: **CODE NAME: PRINCE** by popular author **Valerie Parv** (SR #1516)

On sale June 2001: **AN OFFICER AND A PRINCESS** by award-winning author **Carla Cassidy** (SR #1522)

Available at your favorite retail outlet.

Where love comes alive™

Visit Silhouette at www.eHarlequin.com   SRRW3

#1 *New York Times* bestselling author

NORA ROBERTS

brings you more of the loyal and loving,
tempestuous and tantalizing Stanislaski family.

Coming in February 2001

The Stanislaski Sisters

Natasha and Rachel

Though raised in the Old World traditions of their
family, fiery Natasha Stanislaski and cool, classy
Rachel Stanislaski are ready for a *new* world of love....

*And also available in February 2001 from
Silhouette Special Edition, the newest book in the
heartwarming Stanislaski saga*

CONSIDERING KATE

Natasha and Spencer Kimball's daughter Kate turns her
back on old dreams and returns to her hometown, where
she finds the *man* of her dreams.

Available at your favorite retail outlet.

Where love comes alive™

Silhouette® —

where love comes alive—online...

eHARLEQUIN.com

shop eHarlequin

- ♥ Find all the new Silhouette releases at everyday great discounts.

- ♥ Try before you buy! Read an excerpt from the latest Silhouette novels.

- ♥ Write an online review and share your thoughts with others.

reading room

- ♥ Read our Internet exclusive daily and weekly online serials, or vote in our interactive novel.

- ♥ Talk to other readers about your favorite novels in our Reading Groups.

- ♥ Take our Choose-a-Book quiz to find the series that matches you!

authors' alcove

- ♥ Find out interesting tidbits and details about your favorite authors' lives, interests and writing habits.

- ♥ Ever dreamed of being an author? Enter our Writing Round Robin. The Winning Chapter will be published online! Or review our writing guidelines for submitting your novel.

If you enjoyed what you just read,
then we've got an offer you can't resist!

Take 2 bestselling love stories FREE!

Plus get a FREE surprise gift!

International Bestselling Author

DIANA PALMER

At eighteen, Amanda Carson left
west Texas, family scandal and a man
she was determined to forget. But the Whitehall
empire was vast, and when the powerful family wanted
something, they got it. Now they wanted Amanda—and her
advertising agency. Jace Whitehall, a man Amanda hated and
desired equally, was waiting to finish what began years ago.
Now they must confront searing truths about both their
families. And the very thing that drove Amanda from this
land might be the only thing able to keep her there.

THE Cowboy AND THE Lady

"Nobody tops Diana Palmer."
—Jayne Ann Krentz

Available February 2001 wherever paperbacks are sold!